PRAISE FOR *SPONTANEOUS*

"In range alone, Richard Thomas is b
He is Bradbury. He is Gaiman."

—Chuck Palahniuk, author of *Fight Club*

"Equally devastating and refreshing, this is a collection to be savored by horror fans and literary readers alike."

—*Publishers Weekly*, starred review

"Richard Thomas's *Spontaneous Human Combustion* is a marvelous monster made of blood, anger, fear, guilt, grief, hunger, and pain. These gritty, blood-soaked stories pull readers into the darkness of the single black heart beating at the core of horror and noir, and somehow makes them love every second of it."

—Gabino Iglesias, author of *Coyote Songs*

"Dark, but rarely bleak. Punishing, but never sadistic. Thomas's stories drag you into the light as often as they knock you into the abyss. A necessary collection."

—Doug Murano, Bram-Stoker winning editor of *Behold!: Oddities, Curiosities & Undefinable Wonders*

"Thomas masterfully combines noir and horror. He paints the beauty and the meanness of human life with an ease that belies how damned hard a trick it is to accomplish. *Spontaneous Human Combustion* is a bottle of the top shelf stuff—smooth, but it burns. Burns all the way to the bottom."

—Laird Barron, author of *Swift to Chase*

"Transgressive, dark and masterfully written—with *Spontaneous Human Combustion* Thomas forces the reader to run the gamut of human emotions. With beguiling and devastating prose one can't help but see the beauty in the macabre morsels Thomas has given us to consume. A truly breathtaking collection."

—Ross Jeffery, Bram Stoker Nominated author of *Tome*

"A feast for the senses, this collection is simultaneously lush and terrifying. Horror and dark fantasy fans are sure to find many delights within."

—A.C. Wise, author of *Wendy, Darling*

"Nothing will prepare you for Richard Thomas' stories, for the brutality, for the intense white-hot horror, for the blood-soaked gorgeous beauty of his writing. Reading his fiction is like sinking into a fever dream, filled with an alien-yet-familiar wondrousness to it all that makes you long to be back inside those seductive terrors long after they've ended. I was not prepared: I can't wait to return."

—Livia Llewellyn, author of *Furnace*

"*Transubstantiate* is, is—it's a visual: that 2001 baby opening its eyes in the monolith, but the monolith is shrouded in this story of loss and hope and identity, and encoded in the cadence of that story, if you listen close, is the genetic map with which to draw this impossible celestial infant, opening its eyes on the page, looking right into you."

—Stephen Graham Jones, *The Only Good Indians*

"*Disintegration* is gritty neo-noir; a psycho-sexual descent into an unhinged psyche and an underworld Chicago that could very well stand in for one of the rings of Dante's Hell. Richard Thomas' depraved-doomed-philosopher hitman is your guide. I suggest you do as he says and follow him, if you know what's good for you."

—Paul Tremblay, author of *A Head Full of Ghosts*

"A dark existential thriller of unexpected twists, featuring a drowning man determined to pull the rest of the world under with him. A stunning and vital piece of work."

—Irvine Welsh, author of *Trainspotting*

"Sweet hot hell, Richard Thomas writes like a man possessed, a man on fire, a guy with a gun to his head. And you'll read *Disintegration* like there's a gun to yours, too. A twisted masterpiece."

—Chuck Wendig, author of *Blackbirds*

"This novel is so hard-hitting it should come with its own ice-pack. Richard Thomas is the wild child of Raymond Chandler and Chuck Palahniuk, a neo-noirist who brings to life a gritty, shadow-soaked, bullet-pocked Chicago as the stage for this compulsively readable crime drama."

—Benjamin Percy, author of *The Dead Lands*

SPONTANEOUS
HUMAN
COMBUSTION

SPONTANEOUS HUMAN COMBUSTION

Short Stories

RICHARD THOMAS

Keylight Books
an imprint of Turner Publishing Company
Nashville, Tennessee

www.turnerpublishing.com

Spontaneous Human Combustion

"Repent" was originally published in *Gutted: Beautiful Horror Stories* (Crystal Lake Publishing) in 2016, and is reprinted with permission of the author. "Clown Face" was originally published in *Grease Paint and 45s* (Down & Out Books) in 2019, and is reprinted with permission of the author. "Requital" was originally published in *Lost Highways: Dark Fictions From the Road* (Crystal Lake Publishing) in 2018, and is reprinted with permission of the author. "Battle Not with Monsters" was originally published in *Cemetery Dance* magazine in 2021 and is reprinted with permission of the author. "Saudade" was originally published in *PRISMS* (PS Publishing) in 2021, and is reprinted with permission of the author. "Hiraeth" was originally published in *Behold! Oddities, Curiosities and Undefinable Wonders* (Crystal Lake Publishing) in 2017, and is reprinted with permission of the author. "Nodus Tollens" was originally published in *Deciduous: Tales of Darkness and Horror* in 2017, and is reprinted with permission of the author. "How Not to Come Undone" was originally published in *Blue Monday Review* in 2016, and is reprinted with permission of the author. "From Within" was originally published in *Slave Stories: Scenes from the Slave State* (Omnium Gatherum) in 2015, and is reprinted with permission of the author. "The Caged Bird Sings in a Darkness of Its Own Creation" was originally published in *Shallow Creek* (STORGY) in 2019, and is reprinted with permission of the author. "In His House" was originally published in *The Nightside Codex* (Silent Motorist Media) in 2020, and is reprinted with permission of the author. "Open Waters" was originally published in *When the Clock Strikes 13* (In Your Face Books) in 2019, and is reprinted with permission of the author. "Undone" was originally published in *Gorgon: Stories of Emergence* (Pantheon) in 2019, and is reprinted with permission of the author. "Ring of Fire" was originally published in *The Seven Deadliest* (Cutting Block Books) in 2019, and is reprinted with permission of the author.

Cover and interior art by M.S. Corley
Book design by Tim Holtz

Library of Congress Cataloging-in-Publication Data
Names: Thomas, Richard, 1967- author.
Title: Spontaneous human combustion / Richard Thomas.
Description: First. | Nashville, Tennessee : Turner Publishing, [2022] |
   Identifiers: LCCN 2021026168 (print) | LCCN 2021026169 (ebook) | ISBN
   9781684427550 (hardcover) | ISBN 9781684427543 (paperback) | ISBN
   9781684427567 (ebook)
Subjects: LCGFT: Short stories. | Horror fiction. | Science fiction.
Classification: LCC PS3620.H6387 S76 2022 (print) | LCC PS3620.H6387
   (ebook) | DDC 813/.6--dc23
LC record available at https://lccn.loc.gov/2021026168
LC ebook record available at https://lccn.loc.gov/2021026169

Printed in the United States of America

CONTENTS

INTRODUCTION

BY BRIAN EVENSON

Before I knew Richard Thomas as a writer, I knew him as the editor of a neo-noir anthology called *The New Black*. What intrigued me about that anthology was how expansive his definition of neo-noir was. For Richard, it wasn't simply a matter of contemporary writers imitating the conventions of noir, but of writers using noir and hard-boiled fiction as a springboard to get to their own unique, dark places. Some of these dark places were quite different from what we usually think of when we think of noir. The Weird was part of it, and darkness of various kinds, sometimes crime related and sometimes not. Indeed, many of the stories shaded into horror and the fantastic. From the first story, Stephen Graham Jones' stunning "Father, Son, and Holy Rabbit," I was hooked. What followed were a constellation of well-written stories that went their own distinct direction but still felt like part of a larger, ongoing conversation. The stories were definitely sympathetic with one another, but in a more varied and expansive way than most stories in themed anthologies are. As I read forward, it became clear to me that Richard was much more interested in creating possible spaces for fiction to go than in reining everybody in to fit a narrow definition.

There are two basic ways of approaching fiction. One is to write work that sits primly within accepted genre boundaries but tries to write exceptionally well within those limitations. Such fiction stays politely in its room and doesn't wander out of the house. The other is to grab an axe, chop through the nearest wall, and then use some old warped lumber to connect your house to the house next door. It's transformative, maybe even a little unhinged. As an editor, Richard is decidedly of the second school. Perhaps not surprisingly, he's that as a writer as well, and his fiction is all the more satisfying because of it. If you're looking for typical horror fare, stories that situate themselves squarely in the genre of Horror with a capital H, you've come to the wrong place. Sure, you'll find recognizable bits and pieces from that genre, the ghosts of the tropes you know. Richard knows the horror genre and isn't afraid to use it for his own purposes. But those tropes, those gestures, are deployed differently, are truncated, left suggestive. You'll find instead what Simon Strantzas has called, "the other kind of Horror, the lens of horror," which "is a bit harder to define because by its nature it's undefinable." It's Horror that's "not about tropes, but about intention."[1]

In other words, the tropes, even when he embraces them, are not what give Richard's work its coherence and its momentum. Rather, it's his style, the economy and allusiveness of it, his ability to leave a door open onto the abyss even as a given story comes to a close. It's also the particular way he uses that lens of horror: even when we are quite distant from what might be termed "real life" there are certain things his gaze always drifts back to. Family or intimacy, for instance, as a source of hope and loss and regret and pain. Richard is particularly deft at showing how familial joy and hope is the shining underbelly of the horror. For him, horror

---

1   Simon Strantzas, "Best Left in the Shadows" in the first issue of *Weird Horror* (Fall 2020).

has a more intense affect if it's the inevitable extension of heart-break, guilt, and blame.

For Richard, horror is something that clings to human connection and feeds on it as it dies. What makes these stories resonate for me is that they pry up the loose floorboards of my own fears, particularly the very personal ones, the ones that truly haunt me. These are fears that are deep-seated, almost foundational, because they're so personal. Such fears raise the specter of failure: of my failing those who I'm closest to, of failing myself as well, of failing to be the self I've convinced myself and the world that I am. For many of Richard's characters, it's too late: they were right to be afraid because their world has already collapsed. For others, the sense of impending collapse, their sense (right or wrong) of the inevitability of it, is often enough to drive them away from the very things that give them solace. Sometimes they are so afraid they will destroy what they love that they flee from it in advance, cut themselves off. That, for me, is much more terrifying than the usual horror tropes, such as, say, things that go bump in the night or scary clowns.

All right, I admit it: I'm also afraid of things that go bump in the night. And also scary clowns. And especially scary clowns that go bump in the night. And it'd be remiss of me not to mention that Richard *does* have two scary clown stories in here, but they're different sorts of clown stories than we're used to. One, for instance, puts us in very close proximity to the clown, to his dark and churning mind and then...leaves us there in anticipation of what he is likely to do. The story stops as the darkness within his head prepares to spill out. The other I'll leave you to discover on your own.

Richard opens the collection with a story entitled "Repent", in which a crooked cop seems to be undergoing a sort of failed atonement. "It seems petty now," says the narrator, "looking back, the ways I boiled over, the ways I was betrayed." Indeed it does, once we discover the deal he has made and what he had to sacrifice to make it. There's a way of telling this story that's all plot, but Richard is much more interested in the character's affect, in the emotional damage the narrator is still undergoing. In how this loss makes him feel. And in what, by proxy, this loss can make *us* feel.

Dwelling places are often isolated in Richard's fiction, and shot through with heat. Characters are lonely or alone, either literally or metaphysically. The whole world is permeated with loss and regret. Characters are haunted by what they've done or, in advance, by what they might do. Rage is often bubbling up, threatening to erupt. There are memory gaps, holes. People struggle to remember who they are, experience disorientation from their own bodies (if it really *is* their own body). As one narrator suggests at the beginning of "Nodus Tollens":

> I've been trying to *find myself* for what seems my
> whole life. Now, a dark fate has found me instead. I've
> summoned something; drawn its gaze down upon me.
> This is how the suffering begins.

Suffering, how it begins, how one becomes conscious (even hyperconscious) of the extent of it, and where it leads, is at the heart of Richard's work. It makes his fiction as painfully tender as a bruise. Know thyself, counsels the Delphic maxim, but Richard recognizes that in the quest to know yourself you're as likely to dig something else up, something that would be better left buried. And yet, you can't stop yourself from digging.

These stories are often voice-driven. The voices that drive them are abject, uncomfortable. You might hear some version of them coming out of the mouth of the homeless schizophrenic on the El if you took the time to listen and could understand what he said. Nightmares abound here. There's a story about the feeling of being trapped in a situation that repeats again and again, like a video game gone wrong, and the desperation that comes in trying anything, no matter how extreme, to try to spark a change. Or a story in which the narrator withdraws into a virtual world as his own body and the world around him collapses. Or a story about gambling (kind of), in which the loser ends up having to take on a decades-long burden. There's a brother and sister who seem to be on opposite sides of a teeter-totter: when one thrives the other fades. There's a son's return from a traumatic otherworldly interaction. And much, much more.

Closing the collection is the excellent novelette "Ring of Fire", perhaps the most ambitious piece of fiction in the collection, one that combines an initially mysterious rehabilitation effort with temptation and confusion. The narrator himself isn't quite sure what's happening—even though he often thinks he is—and as a result we have to read the story against its own grain, trying to construct the reality lying behind the story that he tells himself about how this world works. Richard, in this story and several of the others, gives us just enough to energize our reading and drive us forward, but quite smartly opts to leave a certain, crucial amount of mystery intact. This story (and indeed *Spontaneous Human Combustion* as a whole) continues to grow and expand within your head well after you've put the book down.

The stories in *Spontaneous Human Combustion* are quite different from one another. They participate in several other different genres—science fiction, the weird, noir, literature, etc.—at the same time as they always work as slow-burn horror. But despite the range of these stories, they all feel like they were written by

Richard Thomas. Few writers understand misery as well as Richard does, and few are as willing to look with a steady eye at such flawed and suffering humans. Richard has a wonderful ability not to judge in advance, not to dismiss, not to villainize. He's much more interested in zooming in his horror lens to try to see clearly and in vivid detail who people are, to try to understand them in all their abjection, contradiction, and pain. In other words, this is experiential fiction, something to be undergone, lived through. To live through these characters vicariously, with Richard as your guide, will give you a sharper and more empathetic understanding of the darkness of the actual world.

—Brian Evenson,
June 21, 2021
Valencia, CA

This collection is dedicated to every one of you out there who has felt the hateful gaze of bigotry thrust upon them, been treated like something less, been rejected for just being yourself. This is the true horror story. I see you, I value you, I hear you, and I embrace you. Keep going.

"Man is the creature he fears."
   —*BIRD BOX* by Josh Malerman

"When you see beauty in desolation it changes something inside you. Desolation tries to colonize you."
   —*ANNIHILATION* by Jeff VanderMeer

"Old stories told how Weavers would kill each other over aesthetic disagreements, such as whether it was prettier to destroy an army of a thousand men or to leave it be, or whether a particular dandelion should or should not be plucked. For a Weaver, to think was to think aesthetically. To act—to Weave—was to bring about more pleasing patterns. They did not eat physical food: they seemed to subsist on the appreciation of beauty."
   —*PERDIDO STREET STATION* by China Miéville

"What we think is impossible happens all the time."
   —*COME CLOSER* by Sara Gran

I.

REPENT

IN THE BEGINNING, there was no pattern to the sacrifice, merely one more thing to clean up after a long, hard day—no reason to believe that I'd brought this upon myself. No, it was just another violent moment in a series of violent moments—so many mornings waking up in the city, the Chicago skyline vibrating in the distance, my knuckles tacky with dried blood, gently running my fingers over my bare skin looking for bruises, indentations, and soggy bandages. In the kitchen, the sound of laughter—my son and wife crisping some bacon, a million miles away. The decapitated squirrel on my front stoop, I stepped right over it, hardly seeing the fuzzy offering, as I headed out into the snow, boots on, leather coat pulled tight, the bourbon still warm on my tongue, my belly filled with fire. The blue feathers tied into a bouquet, lashed to the wrought-iron fence; they fluttered in the wind, and I barely noticed.

I should have paid more attention.

I huddle close to a metal trash can, the flames licking the rim, my hands covered in dirt and grime, the black hood of my sweatshirt draped over my head like a praying monk, my legs shivering under torn jeans, my skin covered in tiny bite marks, slices up and down my arms, eyes bloodshot, as I hide in the darkness, wondering how much time I have left. I stand at the end of the alley, three walls of faded red brick, eyes darting to the opening down by the street, waiting for something to lurch out of the snow that spills across the sky, the world around me oblivious to my suffering.

I threw it all away.

Perhaps we should start at the beginning.

It's finally time to repent.

• • •

As a boy I liked to work with my hands, helping my old man repair a variety of cars—the '66 Mustang in Candy Apple Red, the '67 Camaro in that shimmering deep Marina Blue. Many a day and night were spent under a car, skinning my hands and arms while trying to wrench off a nut or bolt—oil and cigarettes the only scent. When my father would backhand me over the wrong tool, I'd laugh and grab the right one, as my blood slowly began to boil. It started there, I imagine—the anger, the resentment, the need to transfer that rage. Did I drop a wrench between his fingers, watch it smack him in the face—let the car door bang his hand, step on an outstretched ankle as I walked around the garage? Sure I did. But I never lowered the jack all the way down, letting the weight of the car settle on top of him, crushing him slowly as our black Lab ran around the yard, barking at cardinals and newborn baby rabbits. No, I never let the sledgehammer descend onto whatever limb stuck out from under the cars; I placed it back on the shelf and handed him a screwdriver, a hammer, a socket wrench, and grinned into the darkness.

But the seed had been planted. Yes, it had.

I played baseball all through high school, outfield mostly, and on the days that we took batting practice inside, claustrophobic in a slim netted cage as the rain fell on the ballfields, I'd watch one of the boys pitch me closer and closer, edging me off the plate, laughing to his friend outside the cage, as I started to sweat. I'd squint and tighten my grip, ripping line drives back up the middle, as he kept getting closer and closer until he finally beaned me in the shoulder. The coach watched from a bench on the near wall, chewing his dip, spitting into a plastic cup, a slow grin easing over his face. He loved this kind of shit. They all did. The boy pitched again, and I smashed the ball right back at him, the netting in front of him catching the line drive, a sneer pulling at his upper lip. He pitched me inside, clipping my elbow this time, and I dropped the bat, cursing under my breath. As I slowly walked toward him, massaging my elbow, my arm a jumble of nerves, trying to get the feeling back, the coach said, "That's enough," and my time in the cage was over, the pitcher smirking as he tossed a ball gently into the air, then catching it again, muttering an insincere "Sorry, man" under his breath.

The garden slowly grew.

And the girl—I can't forget the girl. The most stunning blonde I'd ever held in my arms, she was part of my church group, delicate and pale, and as mean as they came. She knew the power she held over young men, and she wielded it like a sword. I did anything she asked—writing her paper for English class, driving her to the mall, giving her money for a movie or clothes, never asking for much in return. She'd laugh as she walked away, but I was oblivious. All I needed was her pressed up against me, a wash of flowery perfume, her lips glossy on mine, her soft, wet tongue sliding inside my mouth as her hand rested on the bulge in my jeans, her blue eyes sparkling as she pulled away. I was hypnotized. Which is why I didn't see them—the others, the phone chirping, her constant distraction—as she kept things relatively chaste between us, while spending nights with other young men. All it took was one party, an event she didn't tell me about, walking around the house with a beer in my hand, searching for her, excited, only to head out onto the back porch, her mouth on his, tongues intertwined, his meaty paws all over her ass, my heart in my throat.

The weeds and flowers commingled, until they slowly became one.

It seems petty now, looking back, the ways I boiled over, the ways I was betrayed. Screws slowly turned into one wheel after another, until the car blew a tire, my father in the hospital—a broken arm and two black eyes, as I stood beside his bed while he slept, shadows in the corner of the room. Funny how a baseball player always seems to carry a bat, one in the trunk, for a quick round at the batting cage, nothing more, of course. I guess that pitcher shouldn't have been trying to buy weed in a sketchy part of town, right? High as a kite, leaning against his shit-brown Nova, a quick rap to the back of the skull, my swing improved, busted kneecap, and his hands now useless for holding much of anything, let alone a baseball, trying to work his curve or slider. Spirits danced in the pooling blood. And the girl—I should have left her alone, I know, but her pretty mouth just set me afire. She liked her drink—it was easy to drop a little something extra in her cup and, later, to undress her so gently, leaving her in the bedroom of that frat house, so perfect in every way. I never touched her, and neither did the other boys. We didn't have to. The rumors were enough. Gibbering words haunted the hallways of our school, ruining her for anyone else.

Up in a corner of my garage lay a bundle of twigs wrapped around a dead mouse—a dull red ribbon and metal wire wringing the wad of hair and fur, holding it tight. At the ballfield, up under the dugout, was a wasp's nest, filled with birdseed and glass shards, a beetle at the center, a singular red hourglass painted on its back. Tucked into my wallet, behind a bent and faded picture of the girl, was a piece of yellowing paper, covered in hieroglyphics, a tree of life in dried blood at the center, my name etched into it with a razor blade. I brought this all on myself, but I never saw it coming.

• • •

Being a cop meant I could channel my rage into official business, and I was good at it, for a very long time. And then I took one shot too many, the kid blending into the darkness, his hands full of something, pointing my way, a gun fired, and then we fired back. In those moments, I was never a father, forgetting the face of my son. It was all a mistake; the kid never held anything but his cell phone, his hands out the window showing surrender, the pop in the night merely firecrackers down the street, my partner and I flying high on cocaine, eager to dispense justice, when none was needed—our offerings hollow and filled with hate. It was over before it began, both of us on the street, and I would have been bitter if it hadn't been a long time coming. It was merely the straw that broke the camel's back—running heads into the door frame of our cruiser, planting drugs on people we didn't like, broken taillights, speeding tickets, young women frisked and violated in so many different ways, backroom deals over packets of white powder, promises made, seething eyes set back into black skulls, curled lips made of brown skin, the glimmer of a badge, the feeling of immortality, and none of it was anything good. I turned a blind eye to pyramids of broken sticks, smoldering leaves and smoking sage, barbed wire and antlers fused to skulls, flesh turned to sinew, bone to dust—evil incarnate, the deeds I'd done manifesting, coming home to roost.

• • •

How quickly I fell, the lies I told to cover up my losses, growing bolder and broader every day.

I had a new job now, fixing the problems of whoever would come to my new office. I'd taken over a crack house down the block from where I used to live, the doors boarded over, the windows too, squatting on the property because the daylight offered me no solutions. I'd sit in the living room, surrounded by torn and beaten-down couches, ashtrays overflowing with cigarette butts, candles burning down to nubs. There was no heat, no electricity, and no water. I had my gun, and a thin layer of filth over my skin, taking what I needed from those that were too weak to fight back, hired out by men and women, drug dealers and cops, tracking me down to my rotting homestead or catching me out at whatever dive bar I could walk to. Around me the ghosts of my family flickered like a television set on its last legs, snow roughing up the faded screen, their voices haunting my every choice.

I'd stay sober long enough to take the pictures, showing the hubby diddling the babysitter; the wife turned to stone, lips tight, a few folded bills tucked into my swollen hands, her mouth opening and closing, chirping like a bird, hesitating, and then asking what it would take for that thing, that finality, not wanting to say it out loud. I'd nod my head and say I could make it happen, but there was no turning back; she'd have to be sure. She'd sip her red wine or her gin or her espresso, and I'd watch the gears turn, the innocence slip out of her flesh, pale skin turning slightly green, her eyes sparking, flecks of flame, the buzzing getting ever louder, her head engulfed in a dark ring of flies, until she opened her mouth, letting the snakes spill out, the deed done, as my heart smoldered black inside my chest. I never said "No."

I'd sit in the back seat of a white Crown Victoria, radio crackling, the men in the front seat wrinkling their noses, the back of the car reeking of vomit, urine, and death. We knew each other once, I imagine, my descent into madness one slow step at a time, so gradual and inevitable that I hardly noticed the noose slipping over my neck, the poisoning so subtle that the bitter taste on my tongue never overtook the lust and hunger, my mouth filled with blood and bourbon, cigarette tar coating it all, as I rotted from the inside out. They'd hand me various things—ammunition, directions, names, addresses, knives, wire, rope, tasers, and envelopes stuffed with cash. Sometimes they would say he was guilty, off on a technicality, a botched Miranda, or nothing but circumstantial evidence. Sometimes they'd talk about witnesses that disappeared, the case ready to go to trial, suddenly the courthouse filled with ghosts—all charges dismissed. And sometimes their silence would fill the car, their dark blue uniforms a color I'd come to hate, nothing said but the place and time, the need for something they couldn't do themselves, telling me to be careful, as they remembered what I used to be, the envelopes thick, telling me to take a shower, Jesus Christ, eyes watering as they tried to look away, tried to pretend I didn't exist.

I felt the same way.

I'd sit in a dark tavern surrounded by other shadows, glassware around me filled with various liquids, amber poured down my throat, one bar as good as the next, the seats on either side of me filled with the shapes of dark acts come to life, filling the space so that no mortal flesh would get anywhere near me, the fumes coming off me like gasoline on a black stretch of tar, shimmering and pungent, not quite solid in my existence. When a hand finally did come to rest on my sleeve, I'd turn to see black beady eyes embedded in a shrinking skull, a red beard flowing off of pockmarked flesh, yellowing teeth uttering threats then demanding answers then asking for help before finally devolving into a long string of begging for something violent. The truth didn't matter much anymore, so I'd take that job, too, sometimes only needing to take a few steps, a pool cue cracked over a head, a knife slid in between ribs while the leather-clad behemoth pissed into the urinal, baring his teeth as he slid to the floor. Sometimes it was a ride into the endless night, the lights of the skyline sparkling like a distant galaxy, deeper into the concrete jungle, or perhaps out into the communities that ring the city, thirty miles north to never-ending cornfields, just to run a blade across a throat, a hole dug in haste, a fire burning late into the night, clothes tossed in, standing naked among the sharp stalks, blood collecting in a pool at my feet.

And yet I still turned away from it all, smiling like a Cheshire cat, laughing at whatever demons lurked inside my melted brain, shadows at the periphery, a flock of birds shooting up into the sky, writhing snakes at my feet, and shattered mirrors whenever I paused to stare too long. Waiting to take my photos, as the windows filled with fog, spiral graphics emerged in the mist, wrapping around the interior of some car I'd stolen, a language I chose to ignore. The cackling radio spit out nonsense as the distracted officers tried to get the case right, hissing and popping noises coming from the interior of the cab, dispatch turning to distant tongues, biblical verse spinning out into the air, *whoever utters the name of the Lord must be put to death.* A cairn of stones was stacked at the end of a dirt road, lost in the suburbs, out past the farms, oak trees ringing the green fields, dusty paths between bulging harvests, and in the middle of the rocks a singular tree branch, forking in all directions, gnarled digits reaching into the sky.

For a man with no faith, it was easy not to believe.

• • •

The things we say when we are desperate—I imagine I said them all. Somewhere between the angst of my youth and the desolation of my last days on this planet, I had a life that mattered. I was in love, and she was able to see beyond the mask I wore, able to lay her hands on mine and calm the savage beast, bring me down off my high that prowling the city streets required. They shimmer like a ripple in the water, my memories of what once was, the boy in his quiet innocence, the ways we used to be a family. It was as plain as can be, a house in the suburbs, with all the essentials—hardwood floors, fireplace for surviving the harsh Chicago winters, bedrooms and baths, a back yard with trees and flowers, a two-car garage, a dog that licked my hand no matter how many times I struck it, a basement unfinished in gray concrete where I'd disappear to in order to shed my skin. We would sit down to dinners of meatloaf, mashed potatoes, and peas, a glass of cold milk, and smiles all around the table, no questions about my day because she knew it had been anything but nice. The first thing she'd do when I got home was to drop whatever she was doing—making dinner, playing with the boy, feeding the dog, working on the computer—just to show me that I mattered, wrapping my weary head in her small, soft hands, kissing my face, hugging me, pressing up against me, to remind me why I worked so hard, her feminine lightness fluttering around me like a butterfly, bringing me down to Earth, pulling my head up out of the ground, as my arms went limp and I tried to shake it all off.

But the death came anyway.

I could lie and say that I'd become a different man, that the wife and son had changed me, made me better, erased my past actions and the violent acts I'd committed. The mannequin I'd become out here walked these streets with a profound selfless-ness, a sense of charity, and hope. And maybe I believed it all at first, that I could repent, that I could ask for forgiveness and find absolution. But deep down I knew it wasn't true. So much had been buried—gunshots in the dead of night, open wounds spill-ing blood and life onto warehouse floors, back alleys swallowing naked flesh and hungry mouths—no, I knew nothing had been forgiven.

Or forgotten.

My memories of fatherhood were fleeting, and scattered, but true. It was like coming up out of an ice-cold lake, skin shimmer-ing, numb yet awake, my heart pounding in my tight ribcage as if it might explode. I could see my son with such clarity, the way he'd wrinkle up his nose or hitch up his shorts as we ran around the back yard kicking a soccer ball, his eyes on me as if spying a dinosaur—something he thought had been extinct, wonder wrapped around disbelief. And then the darkness would come swooping back in, and I'd disappear, my base desires overriding the logic. It wasn't that I didn't see him. I did—but for some rea-son he felt eternal, the time I needed, I wanted, grains of sand in a never-ending hourglass.

When he first got sick, the boy, she took him to one doctor after another, his cough filling the upstairs of our house, his handkerchiefs dotted with yellow phlegm and splotches of red, his skin going translucent as we thought cold, then flu, then pneumonia. Then cancer. I saw how it drained her, how it sucked all of the life out of her, her hair no longer golden, merely straw. Her eyes dimmed to dull metal, the oceans I used to get lost in, shallow and dirty—polluted with worry and exhaustion. She wouldn't even get up from the kitchen table when I came home, merely shifted the wine glass from one hand to the other, her lipstick rimming the glass in a pattern that wanted to be kisses but ended up turning into bites.

And in that moment, I made a deal.

• • •

It was a warehouse on the south side of Chicago—a friend of a friend of a friend—or more like the enemy of a junkie who dealt to some whore, the information sketchy at best, the ways I'd pushed out into the world so vulnerable—a walking, gaping wound, grasping at straws, lighting candles in churches as I stumbled across the city, uttering words that I didn't believe.

Rumors.

Speculation.

The blood moon was a rare occurrence—our planet directly between the sun and moon, Earth's shadow falling on the moon in a total lunar eclipse.

It was a last resort. My time spent praying had fallen on distant deaf ears—knees sore from time spent groveling, fingertips singed from one long matchstick after another, holy water dousing my flesh, as my boy turned slowly into a paper-thin ghost. I told her I might not be back, and she hardly moved, almost as hollowed-out as I was, smoking again, standing in our back yard, her gaze settling on me, finally seeing me for what I was. She didn't have to say that I'd brought this sickness down upon us, for she'd known I was a carrier for as long as we'd been together. She had just chosen to see me now.

I stood over the boy, as he slept, and thought of all the things we'd never done together, and never would. The posters on the walls were of Batman and Superman, and I longed to tell him they didn't exist, to beg him to see the world as I did, which only reminded me of why I had to leave. Even this innocent soul, my son, was just another canvas upon which I needed to splatter my darkness and deceit. Whatever magic and illusion surrounded him, in his youth, why couldn't I just leave it alone? Was I so damaged that the cracks in my armor let all the light out, unable to hold dear a single memory, or loving gesture, or gentle way?

In the corner of his room there was a large stuffed animal, a black-and-white-striped tiger, which I'd won him at Great America, one of the few times we'd spent the day together alone. We rode the roller coasters, ate cotton candy and hot dogs, and then spent whatever money I had on a series of games I told him were certainly rigged. He looked at me with suspicious eyes—unable to believe such a thing could be true. I pointed to the ladder climb, the way it was balanced, nearly impossible to stay on top. A young boy about his age was working his way forward, getting so very close, the guy running the game easing over to the edge of the structure, leaning up against it, and when nobody was looking he nudged the frame, shaking the metal of the game, so the kid spilled onto the cushion below. I nodded my head, but the boy had missed it, squinting his eyes and shaking his head. When we got to the ring toss, I was down to my last ten dollars.

"Nobody ever wins these things, do they?" I asked the chubby girl running the game, her cheeks rosy in the summer heat.

"Sure they do, all the time," she beamed.

"Really?" I asked. "When was the last time somebody won?"

She looked away from me, scrunching up her face, eyes glazing over as she stared off into the distance, searching for a memory that didn't exist.

"See, son," I told him. "Never happens."

He eyeballed me and exhaled.

"Can we try anyway?" he asked.

"Last week," the girl said, "I wasn't here, but Amanda was, she told me . . ."

"Save it for somebody that cares, sister," I said, handing her the bill. She gave us each a bucket of plastic rings, frowning slightly, stepping back out of the way. She swallowed and tried to smile, wishing us good luck, as I glared at her from where I stood.

The boy went through his rings pretty quickly, as I tried to develop a plan, a way to surprise us both and win one of the damn prizes for once in my life. I was working on a backward flip, the rings seeming to clang around the middle of the glass bottles and shoot up into the air. The spin seemed important: not like a Frisbee, spinning round and round, from side to side, but like a coin flip—the motion backward, some new way of beating the system, I thought.

The boy watched me as my bucket emptied, quickly running out of chances.

"See," I said, as he looked on, the day having sapped our energy, the sun starting to set, "this thing is . . ."

And the plastic clinked off the glass bottles, flipped into the air, the revolutions slowing as the voices around us drifted on the hot summer air, the smell of popcorn, my boy smiling, the ring settling over the top of a bottle, rattling back and forth before sitting down for good, staying on the top.

It was a winner. We'd won.

The girl looked at the bottle, back to us, and set off the siren, cranking the handle, yelling, "We have a winner, big winner over here! Winner winner chicken dinner," her smile so wide it ate her face, the kid jumping up and down, and against all logic a grin seeping across my face as well. She asked my son which prize he wanted, and he selected the tiger, almost as big as him, and he took it from the girl, soon to hand it off to me, the day almost gone, the spark of our victory pushing us onward.

"Thanks," I said, as we walked away, the counter crowded with new suckers trying to capture a bit of our luck, the magic we'd had for just a moment.

I stood over the boy and held his hand, a wave of grief washing over me, sitting down, as the tears leaked out of me, sobbing into the darkness, asking the boy for forgiveness, asking my wife for forgiveness, asking God for forgiveness, knowing that none would be coming from any of them—but asking anyway. I'd be gone soon, and it was better this way, if they let me go easy, if they just thought of me as some dark presence that would settle over some other tract of land, a mass of clouds and cold rain, waiting to erupt with lightning and thunder.

I told the kid I loved him, and then I left. I told her the same thing, my wife, and for a moment she was there again, as I whispered my secret in her ear. If I never came back, it meant that I'd won, *we'd won*, and that the boy might possibly be spared. Her eyes lit up for a moment, piercing the darkness.

It was all I had left to offer.

• • •

The warehouse. It's nothing special, but I'm drawn to it like a moth to the flame, and from blocks away, I can tell this is either the worst mistake I've ever made, or the best thing I've ever done. Nobody stands outside the door; a cold rain falls—bits of sleet nipping at my flesh, the possibility of snow. The double doors hang open like a mouth, and inside I see a red glow, an altar in the middle of the room, a pentagram drawn on the floor in white chalk.

I take the three black candles I've brought and bring them to the pile that surrounds the altar, lighting one of them from another, noticing for the first time that the ring of people surrounding the structure are entirely naked. Some are coated in blood, and some are actively violating their flesh, in a variety of ways, a bell ringing from the edge of the structure, a whispering of foreign words filling my ears. A few others at the edge of the room are wearing black robes, the hoods pulled up, no faces to be seen.

I was told to bathe, which goes against all instinct, but I'm clean as a whistle, sweat running in rivulets down my back, the room oddly hot for such a cold day. I undress and stand in the circle, not saying a word. I am not here to question, to cause trouble; I am here to absorb, to pray to dark spirits since the light ones don't seem to care. Incense burns in silver bowls, one on each corner of the altar, the scent of pine and cedar drifting to me, mixed with patchouli, and musk, something sweet cutting through it, a hint of something foul underneath.

A silver chalice is being passed around, something red inside, I'm hoping wine, so I drink from it, the liquid warm and tacky, thinking of the prayers I've come to say, my boy at home, my wife lost to the night, every life I've ever taken dancing in front of me, spirits in a loping chain running circles around the candles. In my hand are slips of paper with the names of my family, my name too, and my wishes for the evening, asking for the disease, asking for the demons to shift, to come to me in my hour of need, to let me become whatever they need me to be, if only they'll spare my wife and child. I've brought this down upon us all, the sickness in me spreading to them. When others step forward to place their prayer scrolls into their candle flames, I do the same.

There is a vibration in the room, as our various mantras are uttered from behind clenched lips and bared teeth, my eyes closed as I repeat the same phrase over and over again: come to me, spare the boy; come to me, spare the boy; come to me, spare the boy; come to me, spare the boy.

A bell rings again in the distance, and three robed men move toward the center of the ring, pulling back their hoods, as they look around the room—bald heads and black eyes, nubs pushing out of their foreheads. When they settle on me, I nod, and they walk toward me, leading me to the altar. I lie down as the room hums, the names of various demons filling the air, and I am reminded of gunshots, the screams of the fallen filling abandoned houses, back alleys, metal wrenching against metal as a car careens off the street into a wall, the sound of feet slapping the pavement, my breath increasing, until it fills my ears. The men place their hands on me, oil coating my flesh, as my skin numbs, coins placed on my eyes as I close them, the tip of a blade placed at my sternum and run down to my navel, my flesh parting, blood seeping over my rib cage and onto the table. I moan, and they are at my ears, whispering, asking, other hands pulling back my flesh, pushing something inside me, and I pass out.

• • •

When I wake, it's dark outside, and I'm sitting behind the wheel of an unmarked sedan, the heater running full blast, the engine rumbling as my partner nudges my shoulder, handing me a cup of coffee. I blink and take it from him, sitting up, as we stare at a set of concrete buildings, Section-8 housing, three people standing out front huffing breath into their hands—a skinny white kid with dreads, a fat black man in sweats, and a skinny Hispanic girl with a skirt so short her ass is hanging out. My partner says we're waiting for somebody to show up, and he goes on about what we'll do later once we bust these punks, some dive bar over in Wicker Park he knows about, cans of Schlitz and a decent pool table, offering me a bump of cocaine on a tiny spoon, which I take, my eyes going wide, a rush over my skin, him mumbling "Thank God neither of us is married." A car pulls up, radio blasting, fat tires on a little car, the bass bumping, and he says it's time to go. So we pull out our pistols, clicking off the safeties, and open the doors, the light inside turned off, slinking in the darkness toward the housing, a whistle and a shout, the skinny kid off like lightning, the girl tripping and falling off to the side of the house, the fat man not moving, just grinning as we rush him, the car speeding off, shots into the wheels, it skidding to the side, stopping, two kids popping out, one taking a shot to the back, the other lost in the night, the big guy raising his hands and whispering don't shoot, but I do anyway.

Somewhere far north of me, a boy coughs and spits and then sits up, able to breathe. His mother sits next to him, patting him on the back, and his color returns, his eyes bright white, a smile slipping over his face, asking for a glass of water. She sees in him something different, and she relaxes for the first time in weeks, months, running her hand over his bald head, holding him to her, the chemo, she says, maybe it's working, a gnawing at the base of her skull, something she forgot to do, somebody she meant to call back, but she can't quite place it, so she lets it go, a phantom of a shape drifting down the hallway, gone forever, a hollow pang in her chest quickly replaced by her boy hugging her, asking about a sandwich now, as the wind and cold whips around the house, a candle downstairs snuffing out, a wisp of smoke curling into the air.

• • •

I stand at the end of the alley and warm my hands. I'm sick. The heat from the trash can barely warms my flesh, the rats running up and down behind the garbage cans, nipping at my skin, and they'll never stop, they'll never go away now. I'm too far gone, a rotten apple bruised and dented, a cockroach at my neck, and I slap it away, eyes forever glued to the end of the brick walls, down toward the light where I can no longer go, no longer any good to anyone, including myself; especially myself. My eyes have become pools of black liquid, running down my sallow cheeks, and I shake my head, trying to focus, but it's no good. I'm blurring now, ready to let go. It will be over soon.

I forgot their names, all of the people, all of the friends, the world around me but especially the boy. His hair was brown, I know that much, his eyes the same, and she was, she was . . . no, I can't remember, she was there, she used to kiss me when I came home, she would hold my face in her hands and try to take my pain. And there were times I let her.

The end of the alleyway fills with bright light, a car passing by, the snow swirling around; and when the shadows drift over the opening, it finally steps into the space I've been watching for weeks, waiting my whole life for, elongated skull and a crown of horns, antlers above its head, lumbering toward me, sinew and muscle, hooved feet clacking on the concrete, great gusts of exhale spewing out of its snout, a flicker of flame, eyes glowing red. There is no pleading now, nothing left to ask for, nothing to forgive.

It shifts its shape as it walks, goat head one moment, minotaur the next, a deep vibration rumbling the walls, the earth, as it laughs a guttural moaning; and before I can say anything, ask anything, it is there, my neck in its hands. A great wingspan unfolds behind it, black as oil, a fluttering as other creatures emerge from under its leathery feathers. There is a pain in my chest as the cancer spreads, filling my chest with a scurry of beetles, my fingernails turning black. My mouth opens as maggots and worms spill out of my gaping last gasp, and I embrace what I have been—the clanking of iron chains, gates slamming shut with a rush of foul wind and a blast of heat. As my eyes close, I see the sculptures, the piles of sticks, the pyramids, the twine and rope, the vines and metal, running up and down the alleyway, these structures I'd been making my whole life, these quiet moments of meditation, sending out into the world a stream of evil that finally added up to something. My pain and pleasure, my suffering and vengeance, a rippling in a dark pond that would infect so many for so long, the waters settling, calming down to a sheet of black ice, the last moments of my rotten life filled with the sound of my son coughing, sitting up, my wife holding him, crying, my name never to be uttered aloud again, by them, or anyone else.

2.

CLOWN FACE

ABOUT AN HOUR OUTSIDE CHICAGO, as you drive north toward Wisconsin, a man sits in the basement of an old farmhouse, wringing his pale, white hands. In fact, his entire nude body is covered in a white dust, a powder, a singular tear running down his right cheek. His overweight body hangs in folds over the edges of his frame, the tiny brown stool beneath him straining under the weight. There is a single light bulb overhead, and it is doing a poor job illuminating the cold concrete, but maybe that's not such a bad thing. For the sake of this moment in time, let's call this man Bob—Bob the Clown. Aside from his chalky existence, the only clue to his occupation is a pile of clothes sitting at the bottom of the long, crooked steps. Let's look over there for a moment, away from the man hunched over in the darkness, and see what we have. A white ruffled top and pants sit nicely folded, a hoop leaned up against the railing,

and under it all a pair of black shoes—you know the kind—
not just big, but *ridiculously* long, triple the size of a normal
man's boot. But Bob is no normal man. No, sir. On top of the
clothes is the only pop of color in the room—a red nose, and a
wig made of rainbows. It's to be expected, these items; the mel-
ancholy that fills the space is something that seems to haunt
men of humor—comedians, and clowns—those who seek to
entertain. Let's look back over at Bob now, and beyond, into the
corner where there is a small metal drain built into the floor,
and overhead, a large shower head, looming like a giant metal
sunflower, dripping cold water to the floor. If we were to ask
Bob what he's thinking about, it would most likely be the last
series of shows—a circus up north, a festival out west, and even
that cornfield downstate. They all blur together these days—
the smell of manure and buttered popcorn, urine and cotton
candy, hay and innocence. He wrings his hands again and then
stands up. Bob hobbles over to the corner, goosebumps rippling across his flesh, and he begins to wash off the cloud of
white, his costume of the day, the way he is able to meander
through any festive occasion with hardly a worry—balloons in
hand, a smile on his face, knots twisting in his gut, blood filling his shoes. The water is freezing on his skin, and he runs his
large meaty hands over his soft fleshy skin, sloughing the white
onto the ground, closing his eyes as the water pours down over
him, sobbing into the darkness. The more he rubs, the more he
washes, the more Bob reveals. He turns in a circle, slowly, wiping, and washing, the floor turning white, as the tougher gray
skin reveals itself underneath, a mottled flesh rising to the surface, the concrete starting to accumulate other items—translucent scales; long, sharp hairs; cracked, rotting fingernails;
and square, browning teeth. No amount of sobbing will change

this molting, this transformation; no amount of pleading, praying, or bartering. When he opens his eyes, searching for some sort of explanation, perhaps, some sort of forgiveness, his eyes turn a dull yellow, a sickness that fills his tainted, swollen eye sockets, spitting blood at his feet, as his mouth fills with razor blades. A whirlwind of voices stuffs his head: screams of children going up and down the rides, roller coasters, and spinning buckets; vendors hawking games and toys; the *clink* of plastic rings against glass milk bottles; the sounds of a band tuning up, guitars and the beat of a drum; a car honking at the edge of a parking lot; a door slamming shut with a dull thud; and names yelled out, *Daddy*; and then the pop of a balloon, the crying of somebody upset, a woman perhaps, maybe a girl, something spilled, somebody hurt, a person lost. Bob tries to breathe, and his chest fills with long, tangled bits of red and orange balloons; bending over, he vomits up pieces of corndog, funnel cake, fabric, and tiny bones. Finger bones—there are so many in the human hand—twenty-seven in total, spilling onto the hard, gray concrete like dice. Finally, he turns off the water, standing still in the quiet, avoiding the waning bulb that swings oh so gently in the cool, musty basement air, instead choosing to lurch toward the corner, and the darkness, squatting now in the shadows, eyes cast to the staircase. Bob is thinking of the future—a day, a week, a month down the road—when he knows he will find himself wandering down a midway, his skin covered in white dust, his hands kneading colorful rubber balloons, a smile drawn on his face, a bulbous nose bright red in the center of his face, his wig a shining beacon of hope and promise, as his gut clenches, and his teeth elongate, all hidden behind the suit, and the shoes, and the laughter. Let's follow his gaze back over to the staircase, and even walk slowly up a bit, to the open door that spills just a touch of sunlight into the expanding darkness, and then out into the kitchen, a radio playing softly on the counter, a window open, the sound of birds chirping, the long grasses blowing in the wind, the corn and soybeans filling the fields as far as the eye can see, to the gray minivan driving up the rock road, dust spilling behind it, shadows dancing in the clouds—lions cavorting, strongmen and bearded ladies, a top hat and tails, and of course, frolicking clowns—and the laughter spilling from the mother, and the boy, the girl, the dog yapping, sticking its head out the window. Bob trembles in the darkness, a large tin of powder and a pink puff waiting for him next to a long, crooked mirror that leans against the basement wall.

Bob is hungry.

3.

REQUITAL

OPEN YOUR EYES, Graysen.

The shack is filling with a heat that rises up from the desert, a weight on my chest slowly spreading to my limbs, as a flicker of this journey unfurls in black-and-white photos, one horrible image after another. My breath is shallow, hard to summon up from the depths, and then I'm sitting upright on the cot, the thin blankets green and itchy, coughing up blood into my open hands. Sand sifts in through the doorframe, the actual wooden door painted red, splintered into sections, and scattered over the front yard. Emaciated, and nude, I squint, looking out through the opening into the pale sunlight, unwilling to turn toward the corners of the empty hut, the shadows filled with memories.

And the girl.

Always the girl.

She smiles in the darkness, blond hair pulled back into pig-tails, red ribbons holding the braids tight. Today it's a light blue dress, ringed with daisies at the waist and collar, her black patent leather shoes buckled, shimmering somehow, the dainty little socks as white as bone. Her hands are behind her back, a grin holding her face intact, and I know what she's hiding. I don't want to see it again, but soon enough she'll show me. Yesterday it was a mad dash into the desert where I collapsed in the blazing sun, dust filling my mouth, my skin turning to parchment.

Today?

The car.

I close my eyes, and I'm flying down the highway, the wind in my hair, the windows open, the beat-up Nova purring across the desolate landscape, the girl and house no longer in the rearview mirror. Jeans and a white T-shirt, scuffed boots, my hands grip the wheel as I push the accelerator down, lunging forward. The blacktop spirals forward like a slick of oil, and I chase it—any-thing to be out of that room, away from her. I click the radio on. Static, up and down the dial, as flashes of faded billboards and dying cactus fill my peripheral vision.

I look in the side mirror, and there's nothing back there. A smile as blood fills the cracks between my teeth, my gut clench-ing suddenly in knots. Under my fingernails, there is so much dirt and grime; I can never seem to get it out. Eyes to the horizon, I cough again, a mist of red spraying the windshield, wiping my mouth as I sneer.

Dammit.

I never smoked a cigarette in my life.

Eyes to the side mirror, the rearview mirror, and the world framed in the windshield shimmers like I'm underwater.

It feels good to be moving.

For a moment, I can almost forget why I'm here.

This particular black-and-white photo comes in several different versions—the grandmother in Alsip growing old and feeble, finally made obsolete; the neighbor hurt on the job, unable to work, abandoned by insurance and company alike; the sister and her addiction, garnering no sympathy, an inability to empathize. But closing my eyes won't help.

I want to be hungry, I want to pull over and order a cheeseburger and fries, a large Coke, at a diner filled with shiny, happy people. I want to say hello to Mabel or Alice and have her smile and put her hand on a cocked hip, call me "Hon" or "Shug," a bell dinging in the window, the counter filled with cowboys, and truck drivers, and that one haggard salesman with his tie loosened, dingy white shirt unbuttoned.

I want it so bad that it aches.

Instead, I get one more photo—and it's Jim from accounting, and his wife. Jennifer? Julie? There are doctors and beeping lights, the cold tile scraped by wheels that squeak, as machines are pushed around, a flurry of footsteps filling the cold, sterile air. There was a child, I was told, but whether it was a boy or a girl, I can't tell you. I should know those details.

If I was anything resembling a human being.

I take a breath, the road unfurling, and yet the desert stays on my right, the horizon forever looming, the mountains to the left quiet in their dismissal.

On that particular day, something was due. It's not important what it was—report, numbers, article, paper, results, opinion, facts. I grip the steering wheel harder, knuckles white, pushing the car down the never-ending highway, that diner always just out of reach.

A sharp pain in my ribs causes me to let go of the wheel, gently massaging the spot, knowing it won't do me any good. A cough rattles into my fist, and I rub the red on my shirt.

Here we go.

What did I say? I can't remember.

I yelled at my secretary; it's coming back now, the desk, the glass windows in the office spilling the city for miles in every direction. My back was to her, as I screamed, face red with rage, fists clenched at my sides. Tan, standing tall, the suit custom-made, the tie special-order, the ring on my left finger platinum, the watch shimmering gold.

Never sick a day in my life.

She pleaded with me.

"Stockholders," I said. "I can't count on Jim."

Her lips pursed.

"You don't understand," I argued.

Rubbing my temples, I never looked at her once.

"Make it happen."

Not long after that, she was a ghost too. Marlie. Or Mary. Dammit. What was her name?

The road turns to the right, as the Chevy hugs the dotted yellow line, and I cough again, slow with my hand, spattering the dashboard, and it's the mirrors again, the road behind me empty, the back seat slowly filling with shadows.

No, not yet.

This one, it hurts less; it's almost bearable. And then it shifts, the pain, my hands curling into claws, as my mouth opens in a silent gasp.

This is how it goes; I know.

I can't hold the wheel, so I ease off the gas, the car drifting to the right, trying to bat at the controls, to keep this ton of steel from veering off the shoulder and into the desert, but this will fail, too, I know, and then we hit something.

Rock, hole, curb, turtle—who the fuck knows?

Doesn't matter.

I'd like to say there was disorientation and then darkness, but not here, not now. That would be a gift.

Out of reflex, I stamp my right foot toward the brake, but it's too late. And then we roll. I push my foot against the floor to try to brace myself as glass shatters, shards embedded in my face and neck, my eyes closed tight. The car dents and shudders, my right leg snapping at the ankle, something pushing into my chest, the steering wheel fracturing my ribs, and then it stops.

I'm briefly granted a respite, the darkness finally slipping in, and for a moment I forget it all. But not for long. It's the pain that brings me back.

The sun fades while I bleed, as I labor for breath, in and out, a stabbing pain when I try to inhale, my hands throbbing, a dull panic all the way to the bone, a whimper escaping my split lips.

When I open my eyes, in the last remnants of daylight, as I count the pulsing horrors that riddle my body, a dozen voices scream out in suffering.

I hear footsteps in the dirt, and gravel, and glance to the open window.

It won't be the cancer that gets me. Maybe not even the accident. And certainly not old age. I see four legs saunter up to the car—gray fur and paws with sharp black nails. I hear a panting that I had thought was in my head, my own struggling for breath; but no, it's something else. The heavy breathing turns to a low growl, and then the four legs turn to eight and then sixteen.

"So, this is how it happens," I laugh.

Points for originality.

And amidst the musky smell of mangy fur and sour urine, I see her black patent leather shoes. The shiny buckle. And the dainty white socks.

And then I smell the gasoline.

When I turn to the window, they're gone.

Out of the frying pan, and into the fire.

There is a spark, and I start screaming.

• • •

Open your eyes, Graysen.

The shack is filling with a heat that rises up from the desert, and I run my fingers over my body searching for the new marks— gently touching my ribs, covering my eyes and feeling my face for cuts, mottled flesh, rotating my ankle in slow little circles.

There is the cot upon which I lie—the same itchy green blankets—and the doorframe open to the elements, sand slipping in, a single red scorpion ambling over the threshold. As always, I am naked, and alone. My lips are cracked, mouth dry, so I sit up and contemplate water. There is a well outside, I think. There used to be, anyway.

"I know," I say to the critter as it skitters toward me. "It's not your fault; it's merely in your nature." It heads between my bare feet and under the cot, to a tiny hole in the back of the room, where it disappears.

Water.

I turn to the corner first, take a deep breath, and nod at the girl.

Today she is in a pair of denim overalls, her feet bare, with a pink T-shirt under the straps, ruffles at the edge of the sleeves, and a silver necklace that looks like a daisy.

Always the daisies.

Her hair is loose today, hanging down past her shoulders, and she smiles a little, eyes on me the entire time, taking a single step toward me. Her hands are still behind her back, but I don't need to see. I've been shown already, so many times.

But I'd like to mark our progress.

She'd like to see me suffer.

Before I can find my way to the well outside, my throat clutching, forcing down a swallow, a tarantula the size of my fist meanders through the door, and I back up a bit, uneasy with the way its legs move, undulating over the faded wood floor, skimming the dust, the hair on its legs making my skin crawl. It looks so meaty—the idea of my bare foot squashing it sends a ripple across my flesh, as my stomach rolls, my top lip pulled back in a snarl.

It follows the path of the scorpion, but this time I pull my feet up, letting it move past me, under the cot, and into the hole in the wall, which seems to have expanded.

Eyes to the girl, but she's gone now.

I'm not surprised. So much work to do.

I stand up, licking my lips again, my swollen tongue gently prodding the cuts and sores that line my mouth, trying to find any moisture at all. The photos spiral into the air, one after another, back to my childhood, fanned out like a hand of cards, as the memories come rushing back. I want to open my eyes, to push the images away; but open or closed, it doesn't matter, as these visions force their way into my mind. The magnifying glass and the ants; the pet hamster set on a record player as it spins around and around; the egg found in a henhouse and squashed, the pale flesh of the embryonic bird wrapped around that singular bulbous blue eye; the cat buried up to its neck, so trusting in its innocence as the riding mower started up; the family dog wolfing down the steak while I waited for the poison to take effect.

And then I hear a woman scream.

The flash of red stands in the doorway—the desert fox still, as if stuffed—black beady eyes on me, ears turning this way and that. It barks once and looks around, as if wondering where it is. It opens its jaw wide again and then screams into the room.

It is unholy.

And then it's gone.

When the rattlesnake slithers into the room, I know there won't be any water for me today, and I can hardly swallow. It's getting difficult to breathe. The snake—tail shaking like a baby's rattle—winds its way across the sandy floor and then darts under the cot and through the hole.

Too easy, I know.

I close my eyes for a second, and when I do, there is a cavalcade of clicking insects scurrying through the door in a wave of tiny bodies. Centipedes in red and brown, beetles with their iridescent shells, a flurry of wasps and bees filling the air with a dull buzz. I cover my eyes and cower in the corner, but they only dance about the room and then disappear.

And then they get larger, the creatures of the desert, progressing up the food chain. A pack of dog-like animals, sniffing and yipping, fill the room in a clutch of mania—coyotes and jackals and wolves circling each other, snapping and tearing out mouthfuls of fur, their eyes wide in a seething mass of hunger and anxiety, as I push back against the wall. They weave in and out, like some biting, dying ocean of gnashing teeth, and yet they hardly seem to notice me at all.

What I'd give for a single glass of water.

What I'd give to not be torn limb from limb.

In their sudden absence, the soft red glow of the sun descending fills the empty doorframe, and a shadow lurches past, a head of horns leaping, and landing, and then leaping again. It passes by, never entering. As I hear the dull thud of its movement push on down the road, it screeches as if caught in a trap, and then suddenly it goes quiet.

When the darkness fills the opening again, it is much larger, blocking out the light, bit by bit, until there is no sunlight left to give. And yet, it still is not in sight. A smell wafts into the room, something thick and meaty, and I gag in the growing night. Whether on two legs or four, hooved or clawed, the thick odor of rotting flesh and fetid liquid spills across the room, filling my mouth with a bitter, itching sensation. It is the smell of burning carapace, the sickly-sweet copper of blood crescendoing across a flat surface, the burning rot of diseased flesh slipping from the bone.

I hold my hand to my mouth and close my eyes, trying to remember the shine of her buckle, the gentle fabric of the pristine sock, as my flesh is painted crimson, skinned alive—flayed for the desert to feed on in primal hunger.

• • •

Open your eyes, Graysen.

The shack is filling with a heat that rises up from the desert, and I do not open my eyes this time. I sob in my solitude, understanding so many things now.

And yet there is more.

I have not been enlightened just yet.

There are depths to be plumbed, dark sparks that were pushed so far down that I thought they'd never see the light of day again.

The girl is here, but I refuse to look at her, whatever romper or summer dress she might be wearing today. Her innocence is a skin that she wraps around her like a snake, ready to shift and molt at a moment's notice.

I can see her anyway, and this time she holds her hands out, something in them, reminding me why we're here.

I don't want to see it.

I won't open my eyes.

"You will," she says.

When the perfume drifts to me, it is as if I have awoken in a field of flowers—a basic pleasure that was taken from me such a long time ago.

It takes me back to my youth.

The citrus is a sharp note in the dry, acrid desert—the orange and plum making my mouth water. The jasmine and rose are a lightness that washes over me, so I inhale deeply, the tension finally unclenching. The patchouli and sandalwood conjure up slick flesh and burning incense, the images spiraling back.

"No, please."

My first love.

I try to sit up, to open my eyes, and yet there is only the darkness. And then I feel her touch.

It is such a simple mercy.

Her hands run over my scarred, withering flesh, and she whispers in my ear, unintelligible words, a cacophony of gentle incoherence. Her eager mouth and gentle tongue press up against my neck, and my heart beats a rabbit-kick in a ribcage crisscrossed with scars.

"What?" she asks. "Speak up—say it again."

She pushes me back down, her lips brushing my mouth, my eyelids, my cheeks, and then she bites, drawing blood. Pushing me down harder, my head strikes the wood of the cot's frame, her mouth at my neck, where the whispers turn to threats.

My eyes are open now, and yet I cannot see.

Her fingernails run down my arms, beads of crimson rising to the top of my leathery flesh, and I am so weak now, so vulnerable.

"No," I say.

"If only it were that simple," she replies.

The photos appear now, in black and white—flashes of skin across so many years, in the back seats of cars, in dingy apartments where beer cans litter the floor, and then later, on glorious sheets made of Egyptian cotton, the thread count in the thousands, instrumental music in the background, candles burning in the muted darkness.

"Not yet," she says.

The others, the same. An echo into the void.

"Not tonight."

"Wait."

"Please."

And the notes change now, to something musky, my stench rising to the surface—the salty tang of panic, my sour mouth gasping fear and confusion layered over shock.

Her hands are so strong, in the dark, and I am vulnerable to her base defilement. She flips me over, her strength growing, as the air grows foul. There is something else with us now, whatever love becomes when it is betrayed, the jasmine wilting, the fruit rotting in a liquid covered by buzzing flies, and she takes from me now what I took from her then.

I plead for her to stop, asking for forgiveness.

But it does me no good.

• • •

Open your eyes, Graysen.

The shack is filling with a heat that rises up from the desert, and the girl holds out her hands, the scroll unfurling, to the floor and out across the empty room, the scripture filled with so very many transgressions.

4.

BATTLE NOT WITH MONSTERS

WHEN THE RED SEA OF RAGE washes over me, I picture a house on a hill, far away from the rest of the world, a band of oak trees around it, full of greenery, a single whisper of smoke drifting up into the sky—a place where nobody will get hurt. It's where I like to go, my safe place, that house on the hill, my skull vibrating with dark thoughts. I find myself sitting in my sterile kitchen; this happens all the time—white cabinets with white countertops and white linoleum floor. Sharp silver blades line up on the Formica table—chef's knife and paring knife, filet knife and cleaver—like soldiers waiting to go off to war, or missiles ready to launch. I am entirely naked, pale skin splotchy and flushed, a splatter of blood on every white surface. Then I blink, and it's all gone. There is nothing to see here; no—not tonight. Out in the back yard, winter pushes ice over everything, trees with skeletal branches reaching to the sky, their screams muted, their voices never heard. A huge metal oil drum sits outside my humble home, in the middle of the concrete pad, flames licking the darkness. Whatever I had been wearing, now reduced to ash.

Later, dressed and showered, not a speck of blood anywhere, my hands shaking, my stomach tied in knots, I vomit into the toilet, pulling a long strand of dark hair out of my mouth, the tickle and itch of its removal running all the way through me. My head is shaved, so I know it's not mine. In the freezer, several packages of meat are wrapped in butcher paper, the red muscle marbled with fat, cut into strange shapes that I don't recognize, no price tag on the loin or flank, no label to tell me where they came from, or what they are.

There was a girl once, who loved me, and her name was Adrienne, with her blond hair like spun gold, her laughter like birds chirping, long slender fingers on my arm, her lips on my neck, the sparkle in her emerald eyes only for me. I don't know when she finally saw it in me, what I did, or how it leaked out, my skin coated in a sheen of sweat, flesh turned to ivory, hands no longer gentle, my eyes dead cold and gone so very far away. She simply disappeared, and I let her go—or so I tell myself when the night closes in around me, and her perfume on my pillow haunts my sleep. In that house upon the hill where I let my skin unravel, where the moon emerges and I fall to all fours, snapping at the insects that hum around my soiled flesh, there lies a crumbling well, and its depth knows no limit, stretching out to the end of time. If I were to put something in there, what might it look like, plummeting toward cold water that it would never find, nestled between the rocks and moss, broken, and silent, and nothing like it once was? Not her, no—not her flesh and blood, simply her memory, and the trigger that caused me to come undone.

That's all it took, my hands on her breasts, our bodies fluid, lips slick with saliva and hunger, one bite too hard, drawing blood, one pinch too sharp, one thrust too deep, her eyes glassy, her neck covered in purple bruises, not knowing when to stop. Her arms around me pulled me in deeper, embracing the pain, wishing to suffer, her nails down my back finally running red, salty sweat stinging, calling for the beast—not knowing what she'd finally awakened. No, I'm sure it didn't take much—one mistake, one painful pleasure just a single step across the line. I saw in her such potential. Perhaps there could have been a child.

The mothers, they always know, with their radar constantly tracking, eyes darting across the playground, scanning the grocery-store aisles, and I smile as I pass them, as they pull their children closer, not knowing why—just instinct, a mother's intuition. I am clean-cut, dressed in proper suburban attire, never stubble or shadows under my eyes, never dirty or wrinkled or drunk. I'm never anything other than a quick smile, a hint of musky cologne, shiny leather boots, and a stylish leather jacket, holding a head of lettuce like it isn't a tiny skull. I drift in and out of their life, in and out of their periphery—a ghost, a fleeting panic, a dark smudge on the windshield of their car. I catch the bouncing ball as it heads to the street, effortlessly, with only one hand, as I stroll about the subdivision, out for a walk in the cooling air. And when I hand it back to the child, and the urchin smiles, eyes tracking up and up, the mother will stand, too, sometimes the father as well, and take a step in my direction. I'll wave them off, the child bounding back, tell them to "Have a good one," or maybe ask "How about this weather?" and on down the street I'll go. See how long it takes, as a solitary male, if you sit on a park bench by the local elementary school, eating a banana with fervor. Hang outside the neighborhood ice cream shop, your gaze holding just a moment too long on the gamboling slender legs of tan girls becoming women. See who is glaring when you raise your eyes back up, their teeth gritting, hands clenched in uncertain fists. Wander through the local toy store and ask some eager young boy, away from his mother just one row over, out of her sight for only a few seconds, about his favorite superhero or which villain he loves to hate, and see how long it takes. How many times have my eyes vibrated in my swollen head as the clerks asked if I needed help, wondered if there was something they could do for me?

Oh, I need help, all right. There's something you can do. Yes. Yes, there is.

"My nephew has a birthday coming up, and I don't know the first thing about age-appropriate toys," I say, and they smile and walk me down the aisle.

There is a singular phrase that echoes upon waking—a line, a question, that bounces off the walls of my steamy shower, lights turned off, sobs filling the dark space as I scrub my skin red, scrub it raw, the bottom of the tub shiny and clean, not a speck or a rivulet, nothing crimson that I can see.

What have I done?

And for that inquiry, I have no answer.

There are gaps in my memory. There are long stretches of black oil that slick over my eyes and block out the sun, eclipse the world—spaces that I cannot fill in, no matter how hard I try. I have no job, and yet there is money. I speak to nobody, and yet there are ripples expanding across my home—lipstick, and panties, and keys. There are bills that arrive, receipts, accounts past due—doctors and lawyers, their faces blank, hands folded, desks littered with pictures of their family, a grin expanding across my tightening face as they turn the frames away from me, away from my prying, lingering gaze.

At the Salvation Army, I lift three garbage bags out of the back of my beige Toyota Camry, a common four-door—as benign as it can get. The first is filled with tennis shoes, boots, and sandals— none of the sizes adult, all of them children, some brand-new, some scuffed and worn, a few falling apart, dried mud upon their soles. The second bag is stuffed to overflowing with teddy bears, fluffy bunnies, penguins, kitty cats, puppies, raccoons, and lions. The third is nothing but blankets, in pink and blue, and as I hand this bag to the boy at the loading dock door, I break down and sob an ugly violence, his eyes wide in abject horror.

"Are you okay, sir?" he asks me, the black bag tearing as I refuse to let it go, his gaze on the blankets, another boy open- ing the other donations, sorting the stuffed animals, dumping the shoes onto a conveyor belt. "Is there something wrong? Did something happen? Did you lose somebody recently?"

And I don't know how to answer him.

I've lost myself.

In my garage, there are twelve shovels. That seems like a few too many. There are long, rectangular blades in black and silver, some skinny, and some closer to square. There are curved spades, with their blades sharp, bent to a point, thin and fat, some brand new, and some rusting with age. There is an entire shelf covered in trowels, every shape and size, tiny rakes with their prongs fac- ing up, a blanket of gloves in green, tan, and gray. Slipping on a pair, they fit my hands as if I'd just taken them off, almost moist; and, raising them to my nose, there is a faint hint of my sweat— earth, salt, and grass. There are no flowers in my back yard, no bulbs buried deep, just waiting to come back to life. But there is also no grass, not in springtime or in summer, the entire space nothing but dirt, turned over, again and again. It is lumpy in spots, freshly tilled here and there, rocks littering the soil, pinecones and needles, garbage drifting over the fence and under the wooden gate—candy wrappers and homework assignments, the paper faded and wrinkled, failing letter-grade barely visible. A squirrel chitters in the tree, dropping its nut, running down to grab it, sniffing the soil, and scampering back up the tree, leaving the acorn behind, jumping from branch to branch, down the telephone lines, and into the neighboring yard.

At the police station they ask me the same question that fills my every waking moment—what have I done? And for them, I have the same answer—I don't know. I beg them to run my fingerprints, to just put me into the system, look at their open cases, missing children, see what comes up—and they take their deep breaths, searching for patience, unwilling to do that, since no crime has been committed. I don't understand—I'm looking to confess. They're trying to get me to leave, and I only want to stay here forever. When I raise my voice, they escort me out the front door, a gentle shove down the sidewalk, faces frowning, their arms crossed. I'm just another unhinged idiot in a long line of unstable jerks. I unzip my pants and start pissing on a squad car, and that seems to get their attention. I'm booked for public urination, and promptly fingerprinted, finally, cackling the entire time, my eyes bulging, their eyebrows furrowed, the Breathalyzer coming back negative—the fingerprints, exactly the same.

It's like a hunger, this disease I carry—something I must feed. When my stomach growls, and I find myself in the fetal position on the living-room floor, begging for forgiveness, empty inside, praying for the pain to go away, the only option is to fill it. There was a time when I was vastly overweight, hiding in the shadows, refusing to come out, the world one endless set of sad eyes after

BATTLE NOT WITH MONSTERS

another, mocking me with frowns and shaking heads, my flesh a rolling wave of disgust. My hunger, my dark traveler, it will not take an apple, blueberry yogurt, a rice cake, or steamed broccoli. It wants meat—gristle and bone, teeth on bleeding flesh, fat and sinew filling my belly, and nothing else will do.

It isn't easy to quiet the voices, when there are so many that are deserving of my attention. A stroll to the park will yield an angry mother, slapping the bare legs of a child, holding his tiny arm up in the air as she does it, her face red and flushed, teeth bared, as his weeping eyes plead at me for salvation. For her or for him, which is it? Who to take? Or the old man with the shaking dog, the poor thing hairless and starving, on the end of a long leash, as far from the bastard as possible, as he kicks at the mutt, cursing at it under his breath, the one thing in the world he can own, and abuse, the only thrill he has left. Or maybe it's a cold beer at the local watering hole, sitting at the bar, nursing a pint of amber ale. If I stay late enough, I won't be the only changeling, her mascara running, hands with red fingernails wandering from one drunken cowboy to the next, his beard and gnarled hands shaking some sense into her, the laughter and spit, the broken glass, and the sharp crack of his hand across her face like a gunshot—and I'm off to the races, hovering in the shadows as the cry of "Last call" pierces the smoky room. But the images dull almost as soon as they're created, a flash of light, and then it all fades to black—the darkness a suffocating presence, which settles in to stay, never leaving.

I wish I could say my work is that of nobility, that I have a higher calling, but that isn't exactly the truth. When the sickness has been spread, both the host and the carrier blacken with decay, the only cure elimination. I am the alpha and the omega, the beginning and the end, my name on the lips of men and women alike, friend and foe, stranger and familiar, asking me to stay for a moment, begging me to leave. Something is fractured; there is a disconnect—electricity failing to jump from one synapse to the next, the dark acts that fill my nights gone by daybreak, the screams and confessions only an echo now.

On the hill, where the house sits, I am not a monster—I am justice incarnate, birthed into this world out of necessity, as crucial as water and air. Not survival of the fittest, simply a thinning of the herd. The old, the weak, and the diseased—they are picked off one by one, the world grown stronger, evolution surely at hand. The laws of nature are greater than the laws of man—*what God hath joined together, this righteous vengeance I wield, let no man put asunder.*

On the days I find myself standing in my basement, the washer and dryer running, bottles of bleach scattered about my feet, plastic tubs of hydrochloric acid stacked against the far wall, a single light bulb swinging back and forth—there is no Bible for me to hold, no words to comfort me, no forgiveness to be given. This concrete bunker keeps many secrets, but I have to confess them here first, reveal myself, in order to be forgiven.

Maybe it's time I stopped lying to myself.

I was blind, and now I can see.

On the day they arrive, no longer laughing, the world around me crystal-clear, the memories spill up and out of the well like a great regurgitation, black snakes writhing across the matted grass. I hold myself in icy confession, arms sliced, fingertips snipped off, the garden shears lying at my feet, tears running down my face, a low wail filling the space. The voices, they are close now, the pounding on the door, the rattling of the window, and I look around my house now, the floor covered in newspaper, my boots by the back door, covered in mud, bloody handprints smeared on the wall, the counter, the table, and my own skin. There are candles embedded in skulls, ringing the end tables, holes drilled through, the wax melting down. A tall lamp in the far corner pitches a weak light through the taut shade, the veins barely visible, thin hairs raised up, a slight scent of burning flesh filling the air. A rat skitters over the empty pizza boxes and Chinese carryout, a finger in its mouth, some glistening jewel sparkling in the gold ring that was left behind, as it passes by, heading out of sight.

When I open my mouth, crimson spills down my chest, all my teeth gone now, the pliers at my feet, several ice cube trays stacked up in the freezer with a single tooth in each slot. The pillows on the faded brown couch are filled with human hair, six of them in various sizes, a tuft of black poking out of one long tear. It is hard to hear now, my two severed ears resting on the glass coffee table, pooling in blood, as my canals fill with liquid, a burning sensation on both sides of my head. And across my gleaming skull, razor-blade cuts weave a cross-stitch that leaks down into my eyes. Flies line the kitchen windowsill, unable to escape, gorging on the waste and ruin, as spiders weave webs in every corner. On the stove a pot of entrails boils, like strings of pork sausage, swollen eyeballs dotting the surface like pale meatballs, the water slowly reducing until it starts to burn, the foul smell turning to smoke. On the chopping block in the center of the table is the abandoned mirepoix—finely diced onions, carrots, and celery—with some thinly sliced tongue. The alarm is going off now, and the doors are cracking in their frames, entry not to be denied. Sirens that were in the distance are so much closer now, on top of me it seems, lights flashing in the windows, blue and red, garbled words shouted into the air, my head ringing, as black spots throb across my vision.

I close my eyes and wait for the bullets—it won't be much longer now.

5.

SAUDADE

WE SET OUT ONCE AGAIN from east to west, water to water, in search of something beyond ourselves, something more. Because this can't be all there is. One foot in front of the other, the luxurious brown leather boots covered in an ashy dust, from the paths we have followed. Created, sometimes. We are an army of one—the voices in my head, the palpitations in my heart, the stress and weather tanning my hide and nearly breaking my spirit. But the horizon is always looming, always promising me something, and I believe.

I *want* to believe.

So I do.

Today it is quiet, and I cross the Mississippi River again, the East Coast an echo behind me now, the West hard to envision, in any form. The others are quiet, resting. A dull ache resonates in my chest, and when I close my eyes, it feels blue. I always imagine it bright in times of happiness and peace, when the nature around me is close and friendly, leaning into cyan. It shifts to indigo when storms roll in, and as the lightning and rain descend, I fade, as always, letting the dark one take over.

We all have our roles to play.

One boot step at a time, jeans faded, fitting like a worn leather glove, part of me now, as reassuring as a cold canteen full of water. I've changed the ball caps on my head as the old ones wear out, starting out Yankees, then along the way Cubs, and as I cross over the metal bridge that spans the shimmering water below, exchanged for Cardinals, the red cheering me up. The things you find along the way, the markers that guide us—I'm always weary, always aware.

Sometimes it matters, and sometimes it does not.

In the middle of the bridge—as the faded metal pushes rusty flakes into tornadoes of misery and contempt—there waits for me a cairn of skulls. It has grown. From behind dark sunglasses, I scan the bridge back and forth, the Gateway Arch fractured in the distance, no longer the bent end of a giant coat hanger, now two ancient metal fingers reaching up in humble acquiescence. I pause for a moment and wait. The sun fades in and out, hiding behind clouds, a cool breeze washing over me. The jaundiced orb appears again, sweat breaking out across my flesh. The faded sleeves of my flannel shirt are rolled up, a colored bracelet of woven twine on my wrist, a memory of something, a friend perhaps. My T-shirt underneath sticks to my back, and I take a deep breath.

I hate this part.

"Howdy, stranger," a voice cackles.

Instinctually I reach to my back and pull the katana out of its sheath, the long blade murmuring encouragement as the metal winks at the ever-bluing sky.

A rift starts to open, a telescoping inside myself that is never comfortable.

"Hush," I murmur to myself. "I can handle this. Let me try."

My ribcage is a flutter of two sets of wings—trapped, but aware. One, white and elegant, coos as my skin ripples with gooseflesh; the other, black as night, yellow gleam watching, cawing as it waits.

My passengers.

My dysfunctional nuclear family.

As the two men stand up from behind the altar, the offering, the sculpture of the dead, they hold weapons in their hands. Bullets are hard to come by these days, my sword a comforting presence, never jamming, or empty, merely an extension of myself. They seem to have had luck scavenging of late, a rifle in the tall, lanky man's hands, black hair in a wild afro. That would be Devin. And a pair of pistols shimmer in Victor's meaty grip, the irony of his name never lost on me.

They don't remember; they never do. But I have to keep trying. The truth is within them—if I can only lure it out.

I stand still, sword in my hands, bouncing ever so lightly on my toes, stretching my calves, ready to move. The guns are probably empty. As I try to calm the turmoil that is slowly building inside me, I feel an elongating, an engorgement of my flesh.

The wolf you feed, that is the wolf that wins.

In that moment, I stretch my arms out, bend my knees, and shrug my shoulders in an effort to relieve the pain, to shake off the shift. My bones become malleable, growing slowly but surely, extending, as my frame expands, as my flesh fills with blood, swelling.

The men blink and step forward anyway. They never want to believe.

"You should go," I say. "There are so few of us left. Try to find a better way in this world."

They laugh and keep walking.

"We seem to have you outnumbered," Victor says, rattling his weapons, "and outmanned." Somehow, even now, in these desperate times, he is overweight—a solid bulk that moves as if his legs were tree trunks, his arms thick branches. He is slow but also dangerous. No remorse, and no hesitation. He continues to move closer, torn tank top that must have been white once, dingy and gray, his mottled white flesh covered in marks.

"Your arms," I ask. "Where did those scars come from?" A grin eases over my face.

He stops walking. Devin, as well. The skinny sidekick squints at me, shaking his head.

"The scars," I prompt. "Quite a few crisscross your flesh. Do they sting? Do they ache? Do they cry out to you now as we stand here, trying to remind you of past mistakes?"

Neither speaks.

"Victor, go. And take Devin with you. I'm just passing through. You can keep your stupid troll bridge. There will be others." I look back over to the Illinois side of the bridge. "Maybe sooner than you think," I say.

Devin opens his mouth, and I almost want to let him speak . . . it would be so interesting to hear what he has to say, for once. But instead, I interrupt. "Devin, do you remember how you got that long line across your face, from the bottom of your pointy chin to the top of your dull, shiny forehead?"

"How do you know our names?" Victor grunts.

The pile of bones shifts, a single skull trickling down, bouncing out onto the concrete, toward us, rattling as it goes. The wind picks up, and the impatience grows, a lurch in my stomach rippling outward. The stench of rotting flesh pushes toward us all, and I step forward, larger than I was a moment ago, two sets of eyes blinking from within.

Devin raises his rifle and fires.

The bullet misses me, ricocheting off metal and concrete with a sharp whine.

"Last chance," I say, walking faster.

Victor raises his pistols and pulls the triggers repeatedly, and the world slows down, my vision fading.

Too late. He's coming.

Arms and legs extending, back broadening, flesh thickening—there is a flicker behind our eyes, and the blade is a blur of metal, the bullets long gone, far down the bridge, passing over, around, and through—leaving no mark.

It will be over soon.

Across and back, up and down, the blade bites, hands first, then across the arms, as Victor's eyes widen, and *now* he remembers. Slicing, separating, up his frame the blade works, the motion slowing down for a single intake of breath before running through him, a mist of blood already in the air, streams flung from the sword, pooling at Victor's feet as his eyes go wide.

"You . . ." he mutters.

The sword is pulled out, as Devin stares on in horror, unable to pull the trigger, everything happening too fast. Victor falls to the ground, to his knees, hands to his gut, holding it all in. With one swift motion, there is a flicker of silver, and Devin drops the rifle, a hush settling over us now, as my grunting and growling dissipate, the top of his skull spinning into the distance. More bones for the boneshaker, more offerings for the dark gods.

A high keening fills our skull, no gasping or pleading, no audible witness to the men's fast demise, only a buzzing, a vibrating, as the white bird steps from claw to claw, bobbing its head, eyes wide, unhappy with my choice.

Shaking my arms, black feathers spill into the air, as I find my breath again, the other one gone now.

I bend over and vomit.

It wouldn't matter what bridge I crossed, or even if it had been a boat. These two men would have been there to greet me. They never listen, and they never run. And in the end, I fail, as I always have, and for that, my eyes fill with tears.

When I have moved their bodies to the pile and taken what I need, I lumber on. I offer a few words to the air, asking for forgiveness, cursing the fates that show me no solution, but to what end?

I don't know.

The blade has been cleaned and returned to its sheath. Across the wood are carvings—places I've been, things I've seen, or done. The tableau grows, filling every inch of the case with mountains, trees, and fire; with soaring birds, howling wolves, and slithering snakes; with hieroglyphics, ancient runes, and intricate patterns. And at the base . . . two simple notches, to respect the dead. I had been doing so well. The first two kills, always here.

I keep going.

I want to make it to a campground I know of, about thirty miles down the road, before it starts to get dark. There is another test coming. I hope we can pass it.

• • •

Down the road is a clearing in the woods, just off I-44 as I continue west. There is a ring of stones, and in the middle of the firepit—ash, layers of ash, so very deep. Stacked to the side is a formidable pile of kindling and logs, dry and easy to break, to burn, so I build a pyramid in the middle of the ring and let my mind empty as I fill it with twigs. I snap branch after branch and toss the pieces into the pile, the sun setting as I build the pyre, waiting for them to show up. The visitors, they won't get here until it's dark, so I have time. Time to gather more wood, to build up the supplies, in case I pass this way again.

Hanging from an oak tree on two long metal spikes is a cast-iron skillet and a dented metal coffeepot. There is a pump not far from here, so I wash them out and fill the pot with water. At the edge of the woods, there is a pile of leaves, branches on top of it, and, just barely visible, a thin rope. I move the branches, brush the leaves away, and pull up on the rope. The lid lifts with a creak and a musty sigh, and I peer inside the wooden box I built some fifteen years ago, lined with plastic, the earth cool inside. I pull out a bag of ground coffee and shake some into the metal filter that rests inside the pot, and then head back over to the pit.

From the pack I carry, I pull out a few supplies—matches to start the fire, and three stringy pieces of meat that have been freshly cut and trimmed, seeping blood into a piece of torn cloth.

I try not to think too hard about it.

The lord giveth, and the lord taketh away.

Taking a quick walk around the camp, I find pieces of newspaper, brown paper bags, and other garbage that has blown across the site. I wad a few pieces into balls, and others I roll tightly as if making a paper log and add them to the kindling.

With the flick of a match, the wood lights quickly, and I sit down on a large log that rests near the pit. I close my eyes and slip away.

• • •

I can smell them before I see them, something sour and mossy. Like a pack of feral dogs, they descend on my camp, lured in by the smell of the cooking meat and the simmering coffee. It is dark now, and I can see their yellow eyes blinking in the woods. I can hear them murmuring to themselves, whispering to each other. When the food is ready, I speak to them.

"I know you're there. It's okay, come on out. I won't hurt you."

There is a shuffling, and they emerge, one at a time, filthy children in all manner of dress—some with jeans and tennis shoes and no shirt; others with grimy T-shirts and long shorts, flip-flops on their feet; the leader in jeans and a faded blue polo, a red bandanna tied around his neck. They are white, black, in shades of gray and brown—not that it matters in the darkness. Mostly they are boys, with a few tough girls mixed in. Some have shaved heads, some long hair; one girl wears pigtails tied up with pink ribbons—the flash of color a punch to my gut. They are all of grade-school age, but not any older. I don't ask their names, because it isn't important now. Maybe later, in a different life, where such things might matter.

"You, bandanna, is this your crew?" I ask, my eyes fixed on the fire.

I know they have weapons—pocketknives, baseball bats, long sticks, and one fat kid at the back with a shovel. I am not worried. They won't come for me.

He doesn't answer me.

"I have food. I've prepared it for you. Because we need to talk, and I need your help."

There is a muffled wave of voices in ears, hands slapping flesh, and a few words drift on the night air to me.

Nohesweirdkillhimyeswhataboutyesthelasttimenowha-tabouthelookslikenohe

"I'm not going to hurt you. There's water at the pump over there," I say, gesturing with my right arm, and in my hand the long blade, the sword reflecting the light of the fire.

They go quiet.

"Yes, this is for my protection. But it's not for you."

Not all of you, anyway.

Again, a murmur, and then the leader speaks.

"We're hungry," he says. "We'll take your offer."

"Comes at a price," I whisper.

"It always does," he sighs, both bent with regret and yet standing tall. He is a flickering shadow, and that's good. We have a chance.

They slowly spread out, and for a second I am nervous, a ripple across my flesh, the white bird fluttering, as the oily crow remains silent.

"I've cut the meat; it's in strips on the rocks by the fire. Wash up, then come over here to warm up and eat. There's only the one tin cup, so you'll have to share the coffee. No milk or sugar, I'm afraid. "

They slowly surround the fire, a buzzing of bees, the boy in the bandanna a reluctant beacon, thrust into a role he didn't want, growing darker every day from the load he carries.

We don't talk.

As they eat—chewing and slurping—I am both disgusted and moved to see them, so few children on the trails, the highways, most already dead, or dying. Often they are in hiding, so I always treasure this moment, as much as I dread the looming task.

I catch eyes on me now and then, the little girl with the freckles, and we share a slight smile in the darkness. A skinny boy with olive skin and cracked glasses that he keeps pushing up his nose, trying to get them to stay in place. And a silent lurching form with a bald head, pale skin, probably the oldest, his mouth left hanging open time and time again. His eyes are dull, bruises on his face, his arms cut and covered in weeping scabs. He is there and not there.

When they have finished, I speak again, my sword by my side. I won't need it.

Yet.

"Things are not what they used to be. We can all agree on that, yes?"

They nod their heads, most of them, anyway, some scratching the dust out of their dirty hair, others picking at their skin or rubbing sore feet.

"The world has gone sour, and we need to repair what we can, set things back on the right path, do what we can to make the choices that will push us forward."

In the distance, branches snap and a limb crashes to the ground. Crickets chirp, a light breeze cooling my skin. Inside, the white bird sits quietly, as the black one tilts its head.

"Do any of you remember me?" I ask.

We've met before. Many times.

The ghost boy with the pale skin, he nods his head slightly but does not speak. He never does. There are glimmers. Eyes go wide and then . . . nothing. Mouths open and then close.

"We've done this before, but the outcome is always the same," I say, and it catches me off guard, the girl with the pigtails, her eyes filling with tears. I sob and cover my mouth. I mutter curses under my breath; tired, so tired—their eyes on me so heavy, and lost.

"I'm sorry," I say.

"What do you want?" the boy with the bandanna asks.

"It's hard to explain, but I've seen things, I know how this will turn out—not just this moment, but others down the road— tomorrow, next week, next month. One of you . . ."

And here I pause, eyes on the children, looking for confirmation.

". . . one of you will betray your pack, and you will all die. It doesn't matter how, or when, or where—it always changes."

Nobody speaks. The wood crackles and spits a spark into the dirt.

"But, if one of you were to make the ultimate sacrifice now . . . here . . . then maybe the future could be changed."

"Who is it?" the girl with the freckles asks.

"That's the tricky part. I don't know."

"What do you mean you don't know?" the fat kid in the back squeals.

"I'm not there when it happens, I only see bits and pieces, the outcome. I can only see shadows, as they come to me in the night, in the darkness."

"How do we know this is true?" the boy with the glasses asks.

I sigh and take a breath.

"I can't prove anything to you. By the time you realize what I'm saying is fact, it'll be too late. You'll all be dead."

The pale boy with the bald head, he nods and grunts. The others look at him, and he claps his hands. He smiles, and it is a horrible thing to witness, his face contorted, bent yellow teeth chipped, or missing entirely. But I hold his gaze and try to smile back.

"He knows," I say.

"This idiot?" the bandanna boy asks. "You know what he's good for? Lifting heavy objects and crapping in the woods. We only keep him around to scare off others. He's useless."

The others start to respond, bickering, questioning him, a slow bubble of noise popping, expanding, a few standing up, fingers pointing, and I don't say a word.

This will never change. The weapons will come out now, I can see them picking up what they have as we speak—knife and bat and shovel. I reach for my blade, but it's not there.

Standing by the fire, one of the kids has my sword, the long blade in his hands, his bald head shimmering in the firelight, a rapturous smile tearing his face in two, as tears stream down his face. Those who aren't standing leap to their feet, and my gut clenches in a flurry of claws and beaks, doubling over in pain, coughing up bile and dead flies—and a single white feather.

The boy holds the sword out, rotating slightly to keep the others away, and then he reverses the blade in a gracious, fluid movement that defies his bruised, broken body, shoving the sword deep into his gut, and out his back.

They scream, kicking up dirt and dust, pandemonium as the boy continues to smile, his eyes gleaming and far away, his trembling hands glued to the hilt, as the life slips out of his trembling body.

My vision blurs, stomach twisted in knots, and, unable to speak, I pass out.

• • •

When I wake up, they are gone. All of them, including the suicide. The blade of my sword is buried in the dirt next to my head, about half of it sticking up out of the earth. There is little evidence that they were even here—boot prints, a few scraps of meat, and a quickly disappearing darkness in the soil: that was the last gift the simple boy left for me.

Perhaps not so simple after all.

Tired, but with a glimmer of hope sparking inside my skull, I walk to the top of a nearby hill, the moon coming out, filling the sky with a pale sorrow. They're out there, I think, walking away from tonight in fear, and disgust, their lack of trust in men reinforced, their lack of hope in humanity doubled. But in a few of the children, there might be something else—a question, a vision of the future.

I sit on the hillside and let it all slip away. Legs crossed, my vision fades again, and I slowly start to levitate, hands on my knees, a blue light glowing from within.

I am drawing attention to myself, and the creatures of the night come closer. But I am unaware, drowning in the feathers of an expanding white bird, a stream of pictures unfurling in front of me, the scent of lavender and pine drifting to me, as the fangs come closer. But I am far away, soaring in the darkness, over the tops of trees, and then mountains, the ocean sparking on the distant horizon.

In my excitement, I have made a mistake.

In my desperation to see *any* other path, I've turned my back on the evil that was lurking nearby all along. One by one, they encircle me, drawn by the light and sparks, eager to destroy that which they don't understand, the wolf that is fed tonight, the one that was patient, waiting for a weakness, to pounce.

And in the black, oily night as my light is dimmed, claws and teeth tearing at flesh, there is a spilling of a great sickness, an unfurling of something rotten into the air. In the silhouette of the glowing moon, a dark shadow expands its wings and soars into the void, torn and broken, trailing black feathers, and a sticky pitch of tar.

• • •

We set out once again from east to west, water to water, in search of something beyond ourselves, something more. Because this can't be all that there is. This time, one set of eyes lurks within, a small blue orb spinning in my outstretched hand, my palm cupping it, as the day unfolds before us.

6.

HIRAETH

DOWN THE RIVER from the struggling village, a tiny house sat at the edge of a massive forest, shrouded in the shadows of oak, pine, and flowering dogwood. There wasn't much on this farm, the land hard and difficult to till, but it was all they had. They grew potatoes, the tubers somehow able to survive, the father a scowling presence in all of his height and bluster; the mother always in another room, busy with anything else; the boy forever expanding the hole that grew inside his chest.

Today the boy would go to town, a cart filled with the misshapen crop, a bent donkey pulling him forward. The father stood with his arms crossed, as he often did, lips moving, a litany of curses whispering into the air. His overalls were stained, the long-sleeved thermal shirt underneath torn in several places, stretched over his biceps, his fingernails grimy with soil. The mother wrung her hands and then wiped them on her apron, her own incantations tumbled into the ear of the exhausted farmer. Sometimes it worked, and sometimes it didn't. To confront him head-on would be unwise.

"Be safe, son," she shouted, waving, as the boy sat down in the wagon, ready to go, to be anywhere but here. "No stopping along the way," she grimaced.

He smiled, turning his head, and waved back. He knew she meant well. And he knew what she meant.

"Be smart, boy, get the full value this time. No bartering for trinkets we don't need to stave off winter."

"Yes, father."

"What does that mean, exactly?" the man asked. His question referenced a familiar rote that he had taught the boy.

"Oil and coin and coal will suffice; canned fruits and vegetables are also nice."

The mother beamed, as the father stared, waiting.

"Go on," he said.

The blue sky clouded over, a few drops of rain pitting the dusty road.

"Toys and games and cards bore fast; barter only for goods that you know will last."

The father nodded. "Go on. Looks like rain."

The boy sighed, cracked the reins, and moved ahead toward the town. He scratched at his flannel shirt, his faded jeans cuffed, dark boots placed on the footrest. The hole in his chest grew, and the young man took a deep breath. Over the hill and down the road, a hedge of thorny bushes held a glistening array of golden fruit. The boy vowed that today he would take one, no matter the cost.

• • •

Finally away from the glare and sharp tongue of his father, the whispering ghost of his frail mother, and the endless rows of festering potatoes, Jimmy cracked his neck, shrugged his shoulders, and took in the land around him. A fire burned in the woods to his right, a single wisp of smoke slipping up into the sky. Hunters, most likely. The land was filled with roaming packs of albino wolves, their pink eyes and tongues the last thing most wandering villagers saw before they were torn limb from limb. Often when he stopped for a piss, stepping to the edge of the forest, he would spy an array of bones, with teeth marks running across them—rodents and rabbits, antelope and deer, even bison and elk at times. Now and then he saw femurs, ribs, and skulls that could only have come from men.

As he crested the hill, the threat of rain still looming, a cool breeze pushed across the land, the scent of pine and cedar filling the air paired with the musky scent of something sweet starting to rot. And at the base of the road, just before the creek and the trembling bridge, the gilly bushes sat in all their glory.

There were many myths and stories told across the land—the albino wolves, which Jimmy had never seen, being just one of them. The rumor he'd heard was that they absorbed the moonlight, and glowed in the darkness, red eyes a beacon in the dark.

Another was that of the Garuda that lurked at the edge of the cliffs to the east, sulking in their caves, diving down to snatch up fish, and wayward children, from the drying lakes. It is said that the Garuda had the body, arms, and legs of a human, but the wings, head, and talons of an eagle. Jimmy didn't believe in them, even though the boy at the market where he was headed today was always waving a giant yellow feather, or two, holding up eggs as large as his head. Ostrich, was what Jimmy thought; that was what he told himself when the nights grew long and empty.

There were stories, too, about bunyip lurking in the swamps down south, bulbous eyes fixed to the front of an elongated head—some versions of the plant with a long, forked tongue, others with yellowing fangs—webbed feet capped by sharp claws, a tail sometimes mentioned with thin, piercing spikes. When the boy and his father went fishing several months ago—a constant stream of curses, exclamations, and insults filling the air—the oddly shaped object they found by the water wasn't a saber tooth, merely petrified wood. That's what his father said.

And there had always been talk of witches in their midst—tales of pale flesh encircling fires under the light of a waning moon; cauldrons bubbling over with exotic spices, herbs, and animal flesh; markings on doors; hushed spells conjured in the darkness of the local pubs, for a fee. But Jimmy didn't believe it.

Not really.

Not much.

Maybe a little.

Maybe now.

He lifted his shirt and ran his long fingers over his bony chest, slipping them gently over the edge of the hole that ran all the way through him. His hands trembled as he poked and prodded, a knot settling into his gut.

• • •

Jimmy paused the wagon, the donkey eager to drink from the stream. He released the beast from its harness and stepped toward the bramble, his eyes darting back and forth, searching for travelers and wandering townspeople. The bushes were off limit and had been for as long as he could remember.

It was forbidden.

The dark vines and branches were nearly black, with veins of chartreuse running through the stalks and leaves. They were ugly, and in fact might have been mistaken for dead if it weren't for two things: the handful of red berries that dotted the bushes, poisonous if eaten, a rash erupting on your skin from their juice; and the startling gleam of the golden fruit that rested in the center of each bush. The gilly fruit was somewhere between an apple and a pear, lumpy and not quite round, with dull orange leaves at the stem. The inside, it had been said, was a garish striping of purple and white, the core a rotten brown, its pulp juicy and sweet.

Jimmy stared at the fruit, eager to take one. He had only two choices—keep his sleeves rolled down and possibly tear them, incurring the eventual wrath of his parents, or push them up and risk the thorns slicing at his skin.

He rolled up his sleeves and went to work, knowing he didn't have much time—for surely another farmer would be along soon. This road was well traveled, the main artery back and forth to the market. Standing close to the prickly bush, he slowly inserted his right arm, reaching for the fruit. If only he could grab it—the flavor, the sweetness, the rumors of its healing properties, the talk of its nourishing meat. The key was to stay balanced, his left hand cocked on his hip, to offset his outstretched arm. Slowly he extended, a long thorn sliding along his wrist, nipping at the flesh, a line of blood drawn up from his skin. He kept going. Bending his arm at the elbow, he turned his head so he could lean his shoulder closer, the branches constricting around his forearm, the space and gap lessening.

"Dammit," he cursed.

The donkey brayed just then, backing away from the water, and the spikes grazed his arm as he shifted, losing his balance. A wagon in the distance was coming closer. He pulled his arm out quickly, cutting and piercing his skin in the process.

"Damn stupid animal," he yelled at the donkey. "I see them coming already."

His arm stung, blood dotting the skin, a gouge across his wrist, shimmering and wet. The wagon approached.

Jimmy walked casually toward the donkey, leading it back to the cart as the wagon slowed and stopped.

"Everything okay, son?" a voice asked.

Jimmy nodded, pretending to struggle with the animal, eyes turned down. "Just fine, thank you. Animal needed a quick drink, but he didn't want to come back to the wagon."

The man nodded, eying the boy. He was in a wagon of his own, the back empty but for a few smashed or rotten pumpkins, his overalls and shirt an echo of the boy's father, the straw hat on top the only embellishment.

"We're off to the market . . . potatoes," Jimmy said, nodding at the back of the wagon, strapping the donkey back into the harness.

"Ay-yup," the farmer said.

When the boy looked up, the man's gaze was on him. "Might want to take care of that arm," the man said. "Won't help your business none when you get to town." The farmer cracked his whip, and the dappled mare snorted, pulling them forward.

The boy looked down; blood ran to his fingertips, dripping into the dirt. With a weary sigh, he walked down to the creek to wash off his arm, a small supply of bandages and cloth tucked into the back of his jeans pocket.

• • •

The market was a success—potatoes sold, all manner of coin, oil, and coal taken in return. A few jars of strawberry jam for his mother, which he knew would please her. Peaches as well. Even a hand-rolled cigarillo for his father, which might go either way—a hand to the back of his head or a grunt and a nod. But Jimmy didn't care. Nobody noticed the bandages poking out from under his sleeve, or if they did, they didn't comment. This sale was a ritual Jimmy performed several times during the harvest, and for once it went off without a hitch.

He had one stop left before he went back home, the bakery for a loaf of fresh bread. He hoped Suki was working today, her long black hair and emerald eyes as much of an attraction as the market, and the store. More so, even. He could smell the bread from here; the decadence.

Tying the donkey to a post out front, he went inside, the handful of coins jangling in his pocket. The bell over the door rang as he stepped inside, his heart pounding in his chest. She stood behind the counter, flour dusting her hands as she rolled out the dough. He could hardly even see the rows of muffins, donuts, rolls, pretzels, bread, and pastries behind her, she was so radiant. Her eyes raised up to him, a smile spreading across her face.

"James, how good to see you." She was the only one who called him that. For a moment, the ache dissipated, and he almost felt whole.

"Hello, Suki. I've come for some baked goods. Do you have any loaves of French bread left?"

Suki wiped her hands on the apron, pushing up the sleeves of her light blue blouse. Her pale skin glowed faintly in the heat of the bakery, cheeks rosy, a forehead dotted with sweat. Mimicking her motion, his own skin flushing, he pushed up his sleeves as well. He stood watching her as she pulled a loaf out from under the counter.

"Last one, just for you."

She eyed his arm and her smile lessened, and he followed her gaze, remembering now.

"Just some scratches from gathering kindling earlier today," he stuttered, pushing his sleeves back down. She handed him the loaf, and he placed a coin in her outstretched hand.

"Be careful," she whispered. "It is forbidden."

"Ah, I don't know what you mean, Suki. Kindling, I said. . . ."

"Your fingertips," she said, nodding her head in his direction.

He looked down and saw that his fingertips were purple, easing into black.

"Oh, my God! This never. . . ." he stopped, eyes to her. The bakery was suddenly too warm, and his stomach lurched.

Suki ran to the front door, flipped the sign to "Closed," and glanced out the window. The streets were quiet, most everyone had gone home already, the market was empty. She'd stayed open late, hoping he'd stop by.

"Come here," she said, taking him by his left hand, leading him into the back.

Jimmy followed her into the dark room, the sun setting now, the last of the dying light slipping in through the open back door. The ovens were oppressive, even as they cooled down, the coals a shimmering glow.

"What are you doing?" he asked.

"Quickly, or you'll lose your fingers, maybe your hand, or arm."

Jimmy quieted, as she pushed him down onto a stool.

"Sit. Be still."

She went to the shelves, searching for something, pulling glass bottles and brown envelopes down, tinctures in various colors, a mortar and pestle, as well as a handful of wild greens out of a vase. She eyed him once, pursing her lips, as she poured powder, then a few drops of amber liquid into the bowl, adding a handful of flowers and seeds. She crushed them all into a paste, dipped her finger into it, tasted it, and then took the potion to him.

"What's this?" he asked.

She didn't speak, only lifted his hand, the fingertips now black, the thumbnail falling to the floor, where it broke into tiny pieces.

Jimmy stared on in horror.

Suki took his hand in hers and rubbed the mixture over his skin, the blackness fading instantly, as her own pale flesh started to darken.

"Your hands," he said.

"It will fade. I have gloves. I'm done today. It will be normal tomorrow."

His own hands tingled, her body close to him, perspiration on her upper lip, eyes wide, as she rubbed, and rubbed, and rubbed.

"Leave the gilly fruit alone," she said. "It's not worth it. It's actually kind of sour."

He stared at her, uncertain how to answer.

Suki turned her right arm over, one little scar running from her elbow to her thumb. It was faint, the thin white line barely visible, even up this close.

"I knew less then than I do now. This is a reminder to me. Some places you just don't want to go."

They looked down, and his hand was back to normal, minus the one nail. Her hands were ashen, the pale gone slightly gray.

"It'll be fine, honest," she said. "But you should go."

Suki leaned over and kissed Jimmy on the lips, and nothing much mattered after that.

• • •

Or so he thought. Standing by the wagon, as the lights clicked off inside, Suki headed the other direction. No need for rumors, no need to spur on talk of their involvement. The village had a mean streak; it liked to see beauty undone. It would remain a secret for now. One of many.

The boy stood by the wagon, staring at the donkey, the beast looking away from him as if in shame.

The cart was empty.

Jimmy's hand went to the necklace around his neck, a simple bauble that Suki had given him, to ward off evil spirits, she had said. To protect him. The leather strap ran through a rough silver coin, a hole drilled through it. On one side there was a griffin stamped into the tarnished metal; the back held an eye in the center of a pentagram.

He hoped it worked.

It was a long ride home, back down the dirt road, the night settling in around him, a movement in the woods that seemed alive. He was late. Stars slipped up into the sky, a harvest moon glowing red in the darkness, the sickness and rage slipping over his flesh. He knew what was coming, and he cursed the town for its petty greed.

The money in his pocket and the loaf of bread, they might save his life.

Or they might not.

He pushed the cart on anyway, headed home, the smattering of glowing fruit to his left mocking him as he rode over the bridge and up the hill to the farm. The coal, the oil, the strawberry jam for his mother, the peaches, and the peace offering smoke for his father.

All gone.

When he stopped in front of the house, his parents were outside before he could even put the donkey away, his mother's eyes gleaming with hope and promise, eager to see what he'd brought back. He walked to the barn and back, and by then her face had slipped into terror, worry for her only son's safety. And there was something else he'd never seen before, a panic that she didn't wear very well. He handed her the loaf of bread and turned to his father, who boiled with rage. Jimmy poured the coins into his hand and looked him in the eye.

"I was robbed. . . ."

And everything went black.

• • •

It took two weeks to recover—broken ribs, broken nose, bruises up and down his arm. He couldn't walk, the bandage undone in the melee, blood staining his shirt, his mother finally stepping in, crying, bawling, as he lay in the dirt twitching. He was no good to them hurt. In fact, they had to work twice as hard now to harvest what was still in the ground, the boy unable to help.

Not one for foresight, the father.

Jimmy couldn't breathe until they left for the market again.

"There might still be strawberry jam," he told his mother. "Peaches, too," he said, tears running down his face.

His mother was stone cold. Not because she didn't love him, but because he had put all of their lives at risk, nearly half of their harvest lost to his moment at the bakery. Neither of his parents blamed the thieves. It was his fault, from start to finish.

"Mother . . ." he began.

She placed a hand on his. She was tired, circles under her eyes, blisters weeping on her hands, lacking the strength to guide the plow, even with the donkey. Muffled noises had continuously slipped from their bedroom in configurations he tried not to imagine.

"I'll look. No need for *all* of us to suffer this winter," she said, a small smile creeping over her face. "I'll start on new blankets as soon as my hands heal. And you'll chop half the forest down before the snow settles in. We won't die on my watch," she said.

She slipped out the front door, and Jimmy heard the whip crack, and they left. For the first time in a fortnight, the tension was gone. He lifted his shirt to look at his ribs, and the hole in his chest glared back at him. As wide as he was, all the way through. They didn't see it—his mother or father—they never had.

• • •

When he opened his eyes, Suki was sitting at the end of his bed.

"What are you doing here?" he asked, sitting up, groaning in pain, and then collapsing back down, his face gone pale.

"Shhhhhhh," she said. "Quiet. I knew your parents would come to town today. I'm home sick. Don't tell anyone."

He smiled.

"I don't have much time. I had to make sure you were alive. I heard what happened. The people of this town, their cruelty knows no end."

She placed her hand on his chest, running her thumb over the coin necklace, and then pulled her hand away.

"What?"

"Lift your shirt."

"What? No, Suki . . . what are you doing?"

She pulled his shirt up and gasped. "My God, what have they done to you?" she asked.

"Broken ribs. I'll be okay."

"No, the other thing. This," she said, placing her hands gently on his stomach, "the hole. This can't stand."

Suki leapt up and went to a bag she had placed at the foot of the bed. She looked at him, paused for a moment, and then carried it back over.

She pulled out a ball of yarn, as large as a watermelon. How it fit into her tiny bag, Jimmy didn't know. She began to unwind it, laying out the different colors. She tied them together, whispering into the strands. "Red is for love, for passion and fire, the flesh of your body, the children you'll sire. Blue is for water, the substance of life, for tears shed in laughter, for husband and wife. Green is prosperity, growth for your soul, let flower and fauna help make you whole. Yellow is sunlight, may it shine down in glory, golden ripe harvest, a fairy tale story."

She continued, tying one piece of yarn to another, every color in her bag. When she was done, she raised up his T-shirt and placed the ball in the hole, where it fit snugly, a wince rippling through his face.

Suki leaned over and kissed him, her hands on his shoulders, as the hole started to shrink, her skin a heady perfume of butter, cinnamon, and a hint of vanilla, her tongue in his mouth sparking emotions for which he had no name.

• • •

Their secret would remain that way. Although his trips to the village were hard to come by, he was a creative boy. He put quite the dent in the forest, clearing trees and fallen branches, piling up wood as high as the house. When his father finally told him to stop, Jimmy asked if he might keep going—sell some of the lumber to help offset their loss. The old man rubbed his grizzled jaw and nodded his head in a reluctant acceptance.

In time, Jimmy would take the timber to the village, again and again, selling it cheap to those with no woodland of their own, but hearths still in need of warmth. Winter was looming, and the coal was long gone, the oil a distant memory, hearty oak and porous hawthorn a welcome gleam of hope.

He would visit Suki when the wagon was empty, sneaking off to the very woods that helped provide his newfound sustenance. They would couple in the darkness, the very blanket his mother made him underneath them, her scent a heady wonder that Jimmy would cling to in the long empty nights back at home.

One night as he was leaving, he found a jar of strawberry jam on the end of the wagon. Two jars of peaches sat next to it. Suki was a generous soul.

Suki was not without her own imperfections—her hands on his waist as she wrapped her legs around his back, their bare skin glimmering in the moonlight. Her fingers slipped to the edge of the hole, caressing the scarred flesh, as he grew larger inside her, a glossy friction between them, his damage something she was drawn to, in measured doses.

In the afterglow, as the stars danced around them, she penned lines of poetry, one strip of paper at a time, conjuring images of gods and goddesses, whispering incantations and ancient fables. The paper was gently slipped into her watering mouth, wadded together into a sticky ball, and then placed gently in the shrinking void, now not much larger than her fist.

Having moved to the village to be with Suki, the trips to the bakery were now on foot, no more chores to be done, his parents unwilling to support his infatuation, no time for such intimacies in their home. The world grew dark around them, but the biting cold of the season was never enough to keep him away from his love. The glow of fire filled the windows of the village, logs burning gently in stove and fireplace alike. Jimmy stood in front of the bakery and stared for a moment at Suki, her belly swollen, her face alight as she hummed under her breath, the baked goods around her a golden wonder.

Jimmy went inside.

• • •

At the edge of the sprawling city, a young man sat on the edge of his mattress, running a thumb over the scars on his left wrist, the itch inside his ribcage convincing him that the quickest path to a solution was not outside, or above, but within. The healing of his flesh held such sweet promise, the release of his own sabotage a heady relief. In his lap, a black cat purred, her emerald gaze quieted, the soft fur under his hand a calming presence. She had not moved in hours. The golden orb outside shone through the open blinds, the translucent drapes pulled back to reveal cars and buses rushing by; children walking home from school, laughter spilling from their lips. There was a chill in the air, winter looming, a sharpness and bite to the wind. On the oak dresser, a vanilla candle had melted down to a puddle of solidifying wax, no longer needed, surrendered to the night. James fingered the coin that rested on his chest, his heart stammering, the leather strap running around his neck, a hint of cinnamon in the air.

James heard a knock at the apartment door, and in his mind's eye he saw another young man—not quite as skinny, not quite as pale—eager to come in, and sit with him, to palaver, deep into the darkness as the night expanded with shimmering stars.

James wrapped his arms around the sleeping cat and stood up.

7.

NODUS TOLLENS

I'D BEEN TRYING TO FIND MYSELF for what seemed like my whole life. Then a dark fate found me instead. I summoned something and drew its gaze down upon me.

This is how the suffering began.

The poker party, an annual event that several friends of mine had been running for many years, is where it started. Once all of our children had grown and left the nests, we found ourselves with time on our hands. Some old rituals we left by the wayside.

Halloween was one of them.

Sure, we'd answer the door. Hand out candy and comment on the costumes. Our displays grew more and more elaborate—tombstones, giant spiders, and hidden scarecrows that suddenly came to life. But once the kids were all gone, Halloween lost some of its fervor. We were bored.

So, we opened ourselves to the universe, asking for entertainment, seeking thrills and oddities to pass the time. I think I wanted distractions from everyday life more than any of the others. My marriage had turned cold after so many years of passion, everything skating across the surface. Maybe I wanted excitement more than the others. It would explain why he chose me, I guess.

That year, the poker party was at Barkley's loft in the city. His place had exposed brick walls and gleaming metal. Barkley's ability to avoid long-term romance afforded a means to a shiny, happy life in downtown Chicago.

Barkley's mustache and goatee made him a contemporary Shaggy without Scooby Doo by his side. When he had a good hand, he'd run his fingers over his chin and stroke his brown whiskers in mock contemplation. Tall and skinny, he was always a good host. His new girlfriend left as we all walked in. Cases of imported beer and bottles of fancy bourbon welcomed us.

Pat was Barkley's opposite, sporting thick black glasses on a slightly pudgy face. He DJ'd in his spare time and always turned us on to new music, and some of the tunes I actually enjoyed. Divorced now, he was full of life and chasing women again as if still in his twenties. He had an affinity for vibrant bowling shirts. His *tell* was squinting his eyes.

John had moved to Indiana to a small town named Dyer. We teased him about that at every opportunity. Dire, indeed. John had been a fan of heavy metal bands back in the day, his long blond locks still an ode to that time, that fantasy, even as his hairline began to recede. John was a photographer. Quite talented, his second marriage landed him one of the models he'd shot years ago. Cliché, I know. But he was happy—as happy as any of us, really.

I would drive in from the suburbs, sometimes in the minivan, feeling embarrassed by the domesticity. Other times I'd take the new Maxima. Its gleaming red shine shouted pride and excitement with the possibilities of what lay ahead.

Like most of the gang, I'd put on a few pounds but was still in pretty good shape. My wife acted jealous when I'd leave for the annual event. Blue jeans, black boots, a dark shirt, and a black leather jacket—it was a uniform I'd worn for many years.

I was a graphic designer, like Barkley. The whole gang had worked in advertising in one form or another. We'd talk about things at the poker game that were related to the industry—Super Bowl ads, the latest hot movie, television shows, billboards, and print ads.

Over time, the game had become monotonous.

I would either win big or go home empty. Barkley tended to lie low until we got good and drunk. Then he'd pounce on the big pots like a puma. Pat would luck into a good hand now and then; always dangerous, it seemed. And John, he'd smile and laugh as he got more and more stoned. His hands and decisions suffered as the night went on.

When I arrived that night, a six-pack of Budweiser in one hand and a bottle of Jim Beam in the other, somebody new had joined our game. He slid in under the guise of friendship and played a game none of us had seen coming.

• • •

We sat around the roughly hewn oak table as the night spun into the darkness. The new guy practically appeared out of nowhere. Tall, with dark hair and pale skin, there was a glint in his eye as if we were all easy pickings. His casual confidence rubbed me the wrong way from the minute we met. At the fridge, it was, as

I added my beer to the stock, shook his hand, and nodded my head. Victor, his name; his grip like a handful of bones.

I remember rubbing my hand after we met and the grin on his face like a jack-o'-lantern; my fingers sore, as my lips peeled back in a snarl.

"Nice to meet you, Victor," I said, as I grabbed a cold beer from my stash. There was always one asshole who was eager to crush your hand; some medieval idea of manliness. "I'm David. Who do you know here?"

He nodded his head toward the table, some vague indication of an invitation—he knew Barkley from some agency. He pivoted quickly by asking me about my boots, where I'd gotten them, and then we were on to some indie film I'd seen, and the question of who he knew forgotten.

In hindsight, that was a mistake. He'd done it to all of us— told Barkley that John had brought him, told Pat that it'd been me, and on and on. Just like that game we played as kids, the looping lie told across many a household as we all stole out into the night, eager to get into trouble—our parents none the wiser.

Victor was personable as we played, and maybe that made it easier. Music drifted out of the speakers as the cards were dealt and beers cracked open. The volume intensified as we teased, made bets, and insulted each other. The night slowly spun out of control as we dug deeply into the whiskey.

On the streets outside, ghosts and witches prowled the city sidewalks. Laughter rose up to us on a cold, wet Halloween night.

What's that story about slowly raising the temperature of the pot so that it eventually boils the frog alive? Yeah, it was something like that.

Victor, oddly enough, didn't win many hands that night. He only sipped at his beverage, barely touching the amber liquid to his lips. At times, when the others weren't looking, I'd see him wipe away a bead of sweat, swallow as if his mouth were full of razor blades, and push down a lump of something that seemed increasingly hard to digest. On occasion his hands would tremble, and he'd take a sip to steady himself. When he turned his head a certain way, my vision growing increasingly impaired, it was as if his skin went translucent—his skull pushing up against the thin flesh—sending a chill washing slowly across my skin. If he caught me looking, he'd wink, then raise his glass at me. I'd smile a forced grin back in his direction.

I didn't like him—not one bit.

• • •

Our games were mostly nickel, dime, and quarter hands of poker—Five-Card Draw, Seven-Card Stud, with a few weird variations tossed in—Baseball, Omaha, even a little Texas Hold 'Em. The rowdiest it would ever get would be the last hand of the night as the clock struck midnight. There wasn't a single trick-or-treater in Barkley's building, and that was part of the reason we let him host. Nobody wanted to trudge all the way to the top of the six-flat. The buzzer at the gate never worked on this night, for some reason. We assumed Barkley disconnected the wires.

At this point in the evening, I was up quite a bit of money. And when I say quite a bit, I probably mean fifty to a hundred dollars. But the last hand, that was always something crazy.

Over the years, we'd bet some stupid things. Sure, the money, all the cash we had in our pockets—that was expected. Sometimes objects of art taken, literally, off the walls. Then the watches were tossed in and sometimes other jewelry. More often than not, the personal items were returned the next day out of guilt.

Other more interesting favors and secrets were sometimes tossed in the pile—a DVD that promised to titillate, quite possibly somebody we knew; a secret stash of drugs—sometimes white powder, sometimes pills, or tabs of LSD. Anything was possible, but it rarely got ugly. The occasionally raised fist or nasty insult forgiven in the light of day. We were friends, after all.

As midnight approached, it was explained to Victor, this last hand, and how there were no limits to what might take place. Raise as much as you want, as often as you want; only one catch to the hand—it had to be here, in hand. No checks tapping into accounts where thousands of dollars may lie; no promises or IOUs that could evaporate come dawn. No, you had to have it on you. No exceptions.

It was a simple hand, with some odd variations—Five-Card Draw, with three draws. That was the first kicker, the extra draws. Next, the wild cards—deuces, because they were the lowest number, and then for tonight, as I dealt the hand, the number *six*. For the five of us, and one departed member, Martin. A picture of Martin rested on a side table, a candle by it, and a warm bottle of Heineken sitting close by. A heart attack had taken Martin, one of the founding members, a few years before.

I paused as I looked at the picture, remembering a night shortly after his death when Martin had appeared at the end of my bed, in shadow, a scowl on his face. I sat up and stared at his thin outline. His eyes were ablaze with anger, hands curled into fists. I thought he might visit me, after he passed, as we'd always said that we'd try to reach out from the other side. But this was not expected. I'd seen too many movies and expected a tearful good-bye and a heartfelt gesture. No, Martin was furious. He had been only fifty-two and not ready to go. Complications from his diabetes took him too soon. I told him I loved him, that I was sorry, and he moved closer. My wife was still asleep next to me. My children were only teenagers then and down the hall in their respective bedrooms.

And then I blinked, and he was gone.

I raised my glass to Martin as I announced the rules. Memories of horse racing, strip clubs, and Cubs games whirring by gave me pause. He was a good man. And sometimes that didn't matter.

I shuffled the cards, and we all ponied up. Our antes tossed in, the cards went around the table. I had a pair of kings, an excellent start, with some garbage alongside it—five, eight, and nine. That hand alone wouldn't get me very far.

The bets went around, quickly going up—five, ten, ending on twenty-five dollars each for the first round. Pretty conservative for the last hand of the night, but we were just getting started.

Three cards for Victor, Pat, and Bark. Two cards for John, and three for me. Peeking under, I saw an ace, a deuce, and a six. Two wild cards and an ace. A full house. Not bad, but not nearly enough for this crazy last hand.

Wait! No . . . four of a kind! Four kings. I smiled inwardly. It might be enough.

The bets went around again, twenty, forty, almost a hundred dollars now.

As the game got heated, John folded, his hand a bunch of garbage. He rewarded himself by lighting a cigar and leaned back in his seat.

Pat and Barkley were still in, and the new guy, Victor, paler than ever, but smiling all the same.

I could try for five of a kind. That was possible with this nutty hand. I asked around first—one for Victor, one for Barkley, one for Pat. All of them trying to improve their hands. Fill that flush or straight. Complete the full house maybe, or take it to four of a kind.

As the dealer, I also took one.

Nothing changed. I'd swapped an ace for a three, no improvement. But still four of a kind, four kings, too. It could win, but it was risky.

"Final bets," I said. "Victor?"

He opened his wallet and pulled out all the cash he had. "Four hundred dollars."

Barkley and Pat stared at him and their modest piles of coins and bills.

Bark took out his wallet, peeked inside, squinted, and put it back in his pocket. He eyeballed us both, took a sip from his beer, and looked around the room. It was quiet, just the faint sounds of the street outside and guitar and bass on the stereo filling in the background noise.

"I fold," Bark said. "Too rich for my blood."

Pat leaned over and whispered to Barkley, who pulled his wallet back out and handed Pat some cash. Pat pushed everything into the middle. "I see your four hundred and raise you two hundred more."

It was six hundred to me. I didn't have six hundred dollars. But I had my car.

"My minivan," I said, the room spinning. "Worth six thousand."

"You can't do that, David," Pat said. "That's too much."

"It's outside. It's here. It counts."

Victor grinned. He reached into his coat pocket and pulled out *his* set of keys.

"Corvette," he whispered. "Look out front."

Pat and I jumped up and ran to the window, looking out across the west loop of Chicago. Down below was an aging red Corvette—still beautiful. Still a classic.

"You're crazy," I said.

"Fuck it. I'm out," Pat said, throwing his cards down and exposing his hand, a jerk move—four queens, with a six—five queens total.

Holy shit, he'd have won. Or at least beaten me.

"Even," Victor said. "That's a call."

"Okay," I said, and I flipped over my cards. "Four kings."

"Goddammit," Pat cursed, and stepped away from the table.

Victor scowled and then slowly revealed his cards.

"You know, I should have gone first. I called," he said. And in the distance, something echoed—a train horn, a door slamming shut, or a trembling in the earth. He had called, all right. And I had answered.

"Straight flush," he said, rolling out the ace of spades, the king of spades, two sixes, and a deuce.

I'd lost.

The room went silent. All eyes to Victor, who grabbed the keys, and the money, then started to leave.

I was sick.

I'd lost hundreds of dollars and my car. I was dead.

"Or. . . ." he said.

"Or?"

"Maybe we can work something out," he said. "Walk me to my car."

• • •

I was still in shock when we stepped outside. The cold wind numbed my exposed skin because I had left my jacket back up in the loft.

Victor stood by the Corvette and looked up at the moon, his hands buried deep inside his pockets.

"I'm so tired," he said.

"Long night," I replied, not understanding then what he meant.

He nodded. "You can have the Corvette. We'll swap. You can win, and you can have the money. I don't need it. I just need you to do me a favor."

I stared at him, squinting.

"What do you mean? What are you talking about? That car is worth a lot of money."

"It doesn't mean anything to me." Victor suddenly *did* look tired. Very tired. His skin seemed to wrinkle. His eyes narrowed.

"I need your help," he said, holding out his hand. In the center of his palm rested an ancient coin. It looked like gold—a two-headed eagle on one side and a pyramid with an eye in the center on the other. He flipped it over in his hand.

I couldn't take my eyes off it.

"Take the car, take the cash, it's probably forty thousand total."

I nodded my head.

"On the first of every month, I need you to flip this coin."

"That's all?" I asked, the city around me quiet now. The cars had disappeared as if we were trapped in a bubble on some slightly different plane.

"Flip it ten times."

"Okay."

"That's it," he said. His eyes watered. "If it comes up heads ten times in a row, then I'll need you to do something for me."

"What?"

"The odds are so long," he said while staring out into the distance of the dark Chicago skyline. Lights flickered here and there. Farther east, the lake shimmered a rippling black liquid below the night.

"I'd need you to kill somebody for me," he said.

"No way, man," I said, stepping away from him. "I'm not doing that."

He took a deep breath.

"Do you know the odds of flipping ten heads in a row? Any idea?" he asked, as his anger rose to the surface and flushed his skin for the first time tonight.

"No, I don't."

"Over a thousand to one, my friend," he said, his voice wavering. "If you flipped this coin every day, it would take almost three years. But once a month, almost eighty-five years," he said. "Or longer. It could take much longer."

"I'm not killing anyone. You're insane," I said.

"Okay. Then you better find a cab. Long way home to the suburbs. What, some thirty miles?"

I took a breath and stared at him. He'd lost his mind. Eighty-five years. I'd be long dead.

"And when you get there, explain to your wife about your car. I know it's just your crappy old minivan, but still, I imagine she won't be impressed."

I paused for a moment and thought.

"Or take the Corvette. It'll be a story you can tell your friends for years. I'll sign the title over to you right now. I'll give you the money. And all you have to do is humor this crazy bastard you met at poker night and flip a fucking coin once a month."

I tried to swallow, my throat suddenly dry.

"What do you have to lose?" he asked.

And I wondered. What *did* I have to lose?

• • •

I wake up with a splitting headache, and the dog downstairs barking at a UPS truck. When I open my eyes, she's sitting on the edge of the bed—my wife, Rebecca. Her brown eyes sparkle, and her long brown hair cascades over her shoulders. She's beaming.

"Have fun last night?" she asks, and smiles.

"I think so," I reply.

"I'd say so," she says, and pours out my cigar box onto the bed. The money spills out. "How much did you win?"

"I'm not sure."

"I am! Almost a thousand dollars! Oh, my God, David."

And she starts kissing me. Her lips go to my neck, her hands to my bare chest, and I suddenly feel sick to my stomach. She runs her hand under the blanket, under my boxer shorts, and I come to life in her grip. I turn my head to the side as she bites into my neck. With my hand on her ass, I press her body up against mine. The coins spill out onto the bed.

And in the middle of them all is a single golden coin. A solitary eye stares up at me.

"Hold on. Hold on," I gasp while pushing her away from me.

"What's the matter?" she says, with worry washing over her face.

"Nothing. Nothing. I just have to hit the bathroom first," I say. "Get undressed," I leer. "I'll be right back."

I walk to the bathroom as slowly as I can without raising suspicion. I close the door and vomit into the toilet.

The coin.

"You okay in there?" she asks. "Don't make me start without you."

I brush my teeth and drink some water.

It's fine. It'll be fine. This is stupid, I tell myself.

I open the door and peel off my boxers.

Rebecca is lying on the bed, naked, her skin glowing, beckoning to me with her hand.

• • •

Later, after we shower and are standing in the driveway, her expression changes. Smashed pumpkins litter the driveway. Our mailbox lies on the ground. But that's not what she's looking at. It's the car. Plans of breakfast have ground to a halt. The car is just too much to be believed.

"So, yeah," I say. "I won a car too."

"From who? You can't take this. Whose is it? Barkley in a mid-life crisis? I know Pat can't afford this. John? Is it John's? Oh, honey, you can't take it from John. . . ."

"No. Somebody else, Rebecca. Somebody new. Victor. Friend of. . . ." and I trail off. "Friend of somebody. Pat's? He works in advertising," I say, and I rub my head. A headache looms.

"You can't keep it," she says. "I don't care if he signed the title over to you. It's not right. It's not *right*, David."

"Okay," I say. "I'll call. I'll get the minivan back," I say. "But how about this . . . breakfast first? I won the car fair and square," I lie. "Let's at least take it for a spin."

She smiles, and I remember why I fell in love with her: that devious grin, the gleam in her eye, and the way she makes me feel alive.

"Well, I don't suppose it'll hurt," she says. And we climb inside.

In my cigar box on the dresser, there is a pile of cash, quarters, and dimes filling the space. And buried underneath it all is a single gold coin that remains unflipped.

• • •

When we get back from breakfast, I spend the rest of the day tracking down the guys from poker. They all share the same response—none of them actually knew Victor, each thinking the other had brought him. I have no way of tracking him down. The name and address on the title lead me nowhere. Eventually, I give up.

Rebecca stands in our kitchen with her hands on her hips, both of us worn out from the excitement of the day. The coffee burbles next to us, brewing a fresh pot. An aspirin container sits on the marble counter with the lid off. I dipped into it several times today, and yet my headache lingers.

I haven't told her about the coin. It is simply one of many in the cigar box upstairs.

Rebecca has gone through the gamut of human emotions— laughing one minute, crying the next; smiling and then her face wilting into a frown; looking away, then back to me, unsure if this is a windfall or a curse. I wish I could tell her the answer. But I can't.

Not then, anyway.

The sun starts to set, and we give up. We choose to accept this fate and embrace the new car. The winnings too. Chalking it up to *one of those things that just happens.*

We settle into our usual positions on the couch, the television flickering as we try to manufacture more laughter. Laughter is the best medicine, of course, for whatever ails us. We hold hands and smile. We hold hands and frown. Eventually, we go up to bed.

As I lie in bed, I can't help but feel that I've forgotten to do something. Maybe it's something I can't quite see, lost in the moments between the fragments of last night, in the gaps between shadows that dance across the walls of our bedroom. A streetlight outside flickers and burns out, and I find myself short of breath. In the middle of the anxiety and questions, I somehow fall asleep. The deal already struck, and the wheels of fate already in motion.

• • •

I take the Corvette to work. Rebecca likes to look at the new car, can't seem to take her eyes off of it, but she won't drive it. Not yesterday. Not today. As it turns out, not ever.

I kiss her and pull her close, both of us blinking, trying to settle into this realm, this plane, unwilling to imagine anything else. It's just a day. A Monday, nothing more. I back out of the driveway, waving at her, and she stands there with her hand on her mouth.

Is she laughing? Crying?

I'm not sure.

She shakes her head and goes back inside, ready to start her day.

I shake my head as I pull out onto side streets, hooking up with a larger road. I head down the highway, a main artery, coffee in the holder, radio blasting, and the thrill of the ride wrapping me up in a cocoon.

Merging onto the highway, I punch it, accelerating across three lanes. Flying down the highway gives me a rush for sure. The buildings and trees blur past as I quickly approach seventy, eighty, ninety miles an hour.

I've never driven a hundred before. So I do.

It feels like I'm floating on a cloud.

In and out of traffic I weave. I'm the asshole for once. People flip me off as I sail past them, their mouths agape, and I just don't care.

I arrive at work, on the north side of the city, twenty minutes early and out of breath. I'm sweating. And, very alive.

The day will creep by after this. How can it not? I'm hesitant to tell anyone in the office what has happened, for fear it will all disappear. I sit at my computer pushing words and images around, selecting fonts, working on a color palette, now and then going to the wall of windows just to see the car outside.

Still there.

On the way home, I drive slower. No rush now as I spent that initial desire on I-94 this morning. I feel a calming bliss as the Corvette hums along, still gliding, as if on air.

I never see him coming. Not from behind or the side. I feel a sudden push to my left, into the center guardrail. I hear the sound of metal tearing, screeching, and I'm bouncing to the right now, clipping another car. Bits of silver, black fly into the air, and then the car spins. There is glass shattering, and I take control of the wheel, straighten it out, and laugh out loud before a wheel explodes. I career into the median, down into the ditch, and through the cables.

The last thing I see is cars rushing toward me. Then I'm airborne, weightless, with the impact surely coming.

• • •

In the hospital, it's quiet and dark. There's nobody with me when my eyes are thrown open by panic, motion, and something else. It's nighttime, the drapes pulled shut, but there's someone in the room with me. Something glides across the tile.

I try to speak, but I can't. There's a tube in my throat, and I start to panic. There is pain radiating out from different places on my body—right knee, left arm, my chest, and my head. The shadow slips up to the bed and places something in my left hand.

I can feel it—it's round, cold at first, but quickly warming up. I know what it is. I remember now. It's what I chose to ignore.

He's gone now. I'm alone, and I can't breathe. Alarms start to go off—steady beeps that increase in frequency. People rush in, all dressed in white, and my eyes flutter as I close my fist. The coin is hidden now.

The last thing I see—Rebecca standing at the end of the bed with tears in her eyes.

• • •

Broken bones, lacerated lung, fractured skull—I'm in bed for several weeks, and then they finally discharge me. I go home.

There was no insurance on the Corvette, of course. I didn't think about it. There was no time. It's a loss—simply gone.

Rebecca is angry. She blames me. If it had been the morning, that first commute, she'd have been right. But the fault wasn't mine.

Well, not really.

But still.

The month has rolled on, and we've hardly talked. She has forgiven me, definitely, but she's still scared. Still angry. I catch her looking at me out of the corner of my eye, lying in bed as I binge on one television series after another. I'm unable to work yet and wake up in the middle of the night screaming about victory, or something like that.

She doesn't understand what's going on.

But I do.

On December 1, I flip the coin.

• • •

I flip that coin ten times the minute Rebecca leaves me alone with my coffee with cream and sugar. I could have stopped at three flips. The first two came up heads and the third tails. But I wasn't sure of the rules, so I flipped it ten times just to be safe.

Then I put the coin back in the cigar box, take a shower, and try not to piss blood.

December turns into January. Our New Year's Eve at home is nice and quiet. We have a few glasses of champagne. My left arm and right leg are still in casts.

And as soon as Rebecca goes to the bathroom, I flip that damn coin, right there on the couch. Heads, heads, heads, heads, tails. And I stop. That's enough. I see how this will go. I understand it now.

Or so I thought.

February, March, April, May, June and I've never flipped heads more than five times in a row. I laugh now when I flip that damn coin, but I flip it on the first of the month, without hesitation and away from Rebecca.

The year spills forward. When Halloween arrives, I fear there will be some kind of anniversary. No poker night this year for me. That part of my life is dead and gone.

We answer the door Halloween night like we used to do, Rebecca and I. Sometimes my back tightens a bit. A knee feels like it might give under my weight, but all manner of ghost and goblin are greeted at our door by a werewolf mask and a slutty pirate. We hold each other as we stand in the doorway. The shadow across the street, it's just another costume to me.

• • •

Five years now, I've been flipping that coin. It's a secret I keep, a monthly ritual that means nothing to me until I flip ten heads in a row.

I didn't even start sweating until the number of heads hit seven. I was sitting on the back porch on a Saturday morning when Rebecca came out before her run to the store.

"You look good today," she says. "I swear, men get better-looking with age."

Before I can tell her she's beautiful, she says, "I'm turning into my mother." She shakes her head.

It's a trap. Say her mother is beautiful, and she'll stare at me with head tipped to one side. Say she isn't, and she'll defend the woman at great length.

"Stay out of trouble," she says—my mouth still open, and I laugh.

I have a coin to flip.

Eight.

Nine.

Ten.

What now?

• • •

It comes in the mail, and I almost throw it out: a plain white envelope with no return address. Something about it makes me stop, forces me to rush inside and hide in the bedroom. I tear it open, slice my finger, sending a drop of blood on the carpet. The slip of paper inside carries only an address. The location is somewhere west of the city.

No date, no name, just the address—1141 Ridgeland Avenue. Somewhere in Oak Park. Nice neighborhood. Old money.

For some reason, I feel like I want to flip the coin. I want to hold it in my hand and feel that odd pulse that's been beating once a month for so many years now.

I can't find the coin, though.

It seems to have disappeared.

I pace the bedroom for fifteen minutes. It's another slow Saturday. Rebecca is visiting her mother. Ironically enough, the two of them are going shopping. I see a Cubs sweatshirt in my near future, and I smile. The little things.

I take the SUV, the five-year-old Pathfinder, and head for Oak Park. I carry a hunting knife in the glove compartment, a baseball bat in the trunk, but I'm unsure of what to do, or how, or why . . . merely wanting this to be over.

It *will* be over, I assume.

And we know what happens when one assumes.

It's a much different ride, this one, into the city. It's an eternity. I text my wife that I'm out to see a movie with a friend. I head south, and then west, numb and sick to my stomach.

The house is beautiful, what they call a painted lady. This house is a Victorian painted in various shades of yellow, gold, and white. The soffit and fascia colors harmonize. Ornate spindles and posts run around the deck. On the top of one spire is a black, metal weathervane shaped like some sort of bird. A raven, perhaps.

With the sun setting around me, I park the car a few blocks away and slink down the sidewalk, between two houses, and around to the back of 1141.

With the baseball bat in my left hand and the knife tucked into my belt, I creep up the back stairs, toward the back porch. The yard is in shadows, not a creak from a step, not a dog bark or wind chime to be heard.

"Come on in, David. I've been expecting you," he says.

I see Victor rise out of a rocking chair and disappear into the house.

• • •

I find myself sitting in a room that can only be described as a parlor—dark wood floors, brown leather chairs, patterned wallpaper, ornate rugs, and crown molding for miles.

Victor sits in a high-backed chair. A smile is on his face. A healthy pour of cognac in a huge glass goblet in his hand. I'm unsure what year it is. He looks exactly the same. Dressed in a dark jacket and slacks with a crisp white shirt. I expect to see an ascot at his neck but am denied this pleasure.

"So do you," he says.

"What?"

"You haven't aged a day either."

He motions to a bar, toward crystal carafes with various dark liquids, a mirror behind it.

My face turns pale and sweaty. My mouth hangs open.

"Sit. Drink. We have a lot to discuss."

I pour something brown into a snifter and sit, the baseball bat still tight in my left hand.

"I'm sorry, David. You were merely one of many. So many years unfurling . . . no end in sight. Every year, every Halloween, I am allowed to recruit one more. This was your time. And it paid off. You're here."

"I don't understand. I'm supposed to kill somebody."

"Yes. It took me a long time to figure it out, David. You're lucky. You have a chance. So many wasted years before I found my way out. So many more spiraling out as I waited for the coins to come up heads. I was stupid, but now you're here. That's all that matters."

He sips the cognac, pulls a cigar from his jacket pocket, and lights it.

"I'm here for you, then," I say, finally getting it.

"Yes, David. You are."

"And then this will be over for me?" I ask.

"Yes. This will be over, your flipping. Done."

But it doesn't sound quite right. I take a few slugs of the liquid, burning all the way down, to settle my nerves. It feels like the poker night all over again. Words and promises. Something off, digging myself in deeper.

If I don't say anything, perhaps I'll be okay. No promises. No binding contracts.

We sit in silence as he smokes his cigar down to the nub. The brandy soon gone, I wait for him to speak again.

"I'm ready, David," he says, and stands.

So many questions. But the end is in sight, and I don't really want to know. I am eager to get home to Rebecca, to be done with this once and for all.

He unbuttons his jacket to reveal the white shirt, parting the cloth to show his pale, bare skin.

"Right here," he says. "The knife should work. No need for guns and noise. No jail cell for you," he says, with a cough.

"That's it?" I ask. "No more flipping? No more killing?"

"No, David. Not for you. The universe will continue on. Others will toil and fail, dark deeds will transpire, promises will still be made and kept . . . and broken, too."

I place the bat on the floor and take out the knife. I'm ready to do this.

"Why me?" I ask.

He shrugs his shoulders. "You were willing."

I stare into his eyes, and they spiral deep and wide. So many years lost in that gaze. Flecks of gold, a hint of smoke, and he smiles, pulling me closer.

"Do it," he whispers. "Please."

And I do.

The knife sinks with ease into his flesh, and a sigh escapes his lips. A shower of coins spills onto the rug at my feet, thudding and clanking into each other.

His smile widens, eyes dim, and the coins keep tumbling out as he crumples in my arm. His flesh turns to dried leather, flaking off, breaking apart. His bones snap as his skull tips back, falling to the ground, where it all turns to ashen dust.

How old *was* he?

And, what have I done?

• • •

He was right about one thing; there was no more coin flipping. For *me*.

Every Halloween I'd seek out my bag of gold coins hidden in the attic, behind decorations and boxes of toys. Behind the Christmas ornaments and old papers. Behind tricycles and year-books. The bag gradually became smaller.

I haunt so many different places now, unable to merely drop a coin in some unsuspecting child's plastic bag or some teen-ager's pocket, caught in the act of egging a house. Not that I would do that. No, the act must be complicit. There must be a verbal agreement. And it can only be struck once a year, on Halloween.

For a while, we did it together. Rebecca and I, cruising parties and nightclubs. My sudden interest in the holiday surprising to her, after all that we'd been through together.

"Let's take back the night," I said. And we did. We tried to. My wagers and coins were placed in palms all over Chicago—Wicker Park, Evanston, Pilsen, and Oak Park. I was a magician, a gambler, a pirate, and a prophet. But the coins, they still haunted me.

She's been gone for many years now, my Rebecca. Only wise to my antics as we neared the end. Instead of dying my hair to look younger, I did exactly the opposite to fit in. I aged myself in every possible way, but she saw through it.

"What did you promise?" she asked me, lying in bed, as the last of her life slipped away.

"Too much," I said.

It's time again, Halloween. The old Victorian? She is my last true love. I've come to embrace her, as I imagine Victor did. He gave her to me, as she was given to him, so many years ago. I will answer the door. I will keep an eye out for a wandering father in search of a spirited wager. I will turn out the lights and find my way to my old stomping grounds, where other bets and gambling will transpire. And I will hand out a single coin with a two-headed eagle on one side and a pyramid encasing a single eye on the other.

And they will flip their coins, and I will wait.

For the knock to come.

For the knife to incise.

For the disease to finally be passed on.

8.

HOW NOT TO COME UNDONE

THE FAMILY HEARD that the meteor shower would be visible from the cornfields of northern Illinois, just twenty minutes away from their sedentary suburban bliss, but Robert had been sleepless for weeks already, images flickering across his dreams—shadows and voices, a burning sensation running all the way to his core. They were mother and father, sister and brother—nothing special, rows of houses the same, but in blue, or yellow, or brick. But for the boy, half of a set of twins, all the magic and wonder rested in his cells—the darkness and vengeance in his sister, Rachel. So as they snuffed out the lights of the family sedan, hand in hand down a dirt path the boy had mapped out, trust so easy to come by in this family—the girl sparked danger in her squinting eyes, as the boy's ever widened to the stars, and possibility. Fresh-cut grass lingered under buzzing power lines that disappeared as they stretched out to the horizon, a moist smell ripe with cleanliness and godliness—a hint of something sour underneath. The girl grinned as the rest held their noses, so eager was she to embrace death.

There was little talking, words so often failing them—the father full of muscle and pride, a quick arm around them all, a comforting presence on most days. The mother overflowing with worry, her long black hair often charged with static, as if thought and trembling nerves bubbled up to the surface of her pulsating skull. They did their best. And as the dry grasses and weeds rose up around them, they held hands again, while the twins parted, spying each other, mother and father taking a breath together, searching for peace. They had spoken of meteors, talked about aliens, listed off planets—space so wide and unforgiving. Such potential, still, and yet so much that was unknown, unimaginable. In each of them a different static, signals from far away mumbling *welcome*, whispering *promise*, giggling *failure*.

At the top of a hill, they stopped, a blanket unfurled, some of them sighing, others grimacing in pain. The questions they would ask themselves on nights like this, and were in fact contemplating at this very moment, ran the gamut from inspired to self-destructive. Why me? Why *not* me? What does it all matter? Why are we *here*? On the darker nights when children lay healing, or feverish, or sick with disease, the father might pray a little—ask for the burden all to himself, willing to eat such pain with hardly a hesitation. On the darker nights, the mother asked for forgiveness—somehow feeling that it must surely be her fault. Both asking quiet gods to pass over their twins, to find their sacrifice elsewhere. The boy might lie staring at his sister, the room black around them but for a singular bulb in the closet, her eyes as dark as coal, yet shimmering all the same.

"Rachel, don't," he'd say.

"What?" she might reply.

"Any of it," he whispered, pausing. "All of it."

But he knew what she was, what she would become; and no matter his hope, his spark, there was little he could really do.

Or so he thought.

In the grass, on the hill, they scanned the sky for falling stars, for meteors, bits of fire and light and danger. The father fell asleep first, one last deep breath, searching his mind for the answer to so many questions, unable to quite figure it out before he went silent. It was like this on most nights—but then again, some evenings he solved many a riddle. The mother felt her husband go, and let it happen, the weight of it all just too much to carry, letting worry run off of her like rain on a slicker, giving in to weakness, expecting only the worst. But it rarely came. The girl had been waiting for this, the parents to slip away into slumber, for the darkness was calling to her, from every corner of the field.

"No, don't," the boy said.

"What?" she laughed.

"Any of it," he sighed. "All of it. Please. No. Let it be."

She batted her eyes, as if confused, and then lowered her gaze, incantations slipping over her lips, as the wind picked up, fireflies dancing on the breeze, a faint brush of lavender from the bushes back by the car.

But the boy was curious, and so he propped himself up on his elbows, the night full of so much curiosity—why not her? Maybe he was wrong. He could be wrong.

She found a stick and broke it into pieces, quickly stacking the twigs on a flat rock that sat exposed to the moonlight, forming the wooden splinters into a triangle, and then a pyramid, crossing one over the other, pulling a clover with four leaves from the grass, running a sharp thumbnail over her scarred palm, drops of crimson falling to the stone.

"No," Robert said, standing up, his parent oblivious as if spellbound. "Not like that."

"This is the moment you always get queasy, brother," she whispered. "Not all that glitters is gold," she said, staring at the moon, baring her long, white neck as the boy took a step toward her.

"Must it always be death?" he asked.

"No," she said, bowing her head, as if that were the only trick she knew.

A flash of light overhead and his eyes shot toward the heavens, black felt dotted with pinpricks, slashes and sparks darting right to left, right to left, disappearing and fading over the hills and into the distance.

"So it begins," he said, embracing what she'd set in motion.

"I don't think that's me, brother," she laughed.

He spread his arms wide, as the stars fell around them, filling the sky, but so very far away. To the horizon it was as if they might land upon them, but no, that wouldn't happen. Couldn't happen.

If she had asked for death, then what had he asked for?

Evoking a crucifix, he opened his palms, and stardust fell upon them, as their eyes grew wide, a distant spark growing closer and closer until it lit up the field, the two of them trembling, his right hand catching something red.

He brought his hands together, the left hand over the right fist, a heat inside, bouncing and struggling, his hands glowing yellow beneath the flesh, orange seeping out. The girl came closer, smiling wide, the boy trembling, skin gone pale, sick, and uncertain.

What had he done?

"Open your hands," she asked.

"No, I can't," he said.

"You must."

And so he did.

It glowed and pulsed, voices like underwater mumbling, a dark sphere spinning and rolling, spilling into itself, some sort of question being asked—forgiveness, perhaps, favor maybe, unable to breathe, his mouth open wide.

Without thinking, he swallowed it down, hands to his mouth, as it burned and healed down his throat, burned and sealed as it descended, as it burrowed deeper, filling his body with light, rays pouring out of his mouth, his nostrils, his ears, leaking out of his eyes—arms wide, his sister stepping back in shock, his chest thrust out, neck bent back, and then it was over.

Darkness again.

The boy collapsed.

The girl grinned.

And the parents woke up.

It was only the beginning.

● ● ●

After that, things were different.

The summer unspooled like a giant ball of twine, the boy glowing everywhere he went, his skin tan, eyes sparkling, his brown hair more blond every day. And the girl, just the opposite, pale to the point of translucence, her eyes two black orbs, her fingernails bitten to jagged daggers.

As long as they had been aware of each other, and possibly even before that, the twins had balanced each other out in so many different ways—yin and yang, dark and light, day and night. Things were more established now, nearly teens, the concrete nearly set, but it hadn't always been that way. The balance, it had been fluid. When Robert was joyful, Rachel became angry. When the boy fell ill, the girl danced around the house, trying to cheer him, full of life. The best they could wish for was a rare neutral state where neither was happy or sad, just present—equal. And that was no way to live a life. Was it?

The family didn't talk about the meteors, the light show, what might have happened. It was a buried secret that no one ever brought up. Partly, the parents felt responsible, no surprise, and partly they didn't believe. But the twins knew, and their eyes lingered on each other, opening their mouths to speak, like baby birds eager for a worm, only to snap shut. Quiet. Uncertain.

More and more the boy would find himself sitting on the front porch of their house, Chicago brick, split with wooden frames, windows facing out in all directions, enough of a yard to run around. Rachel would find him sitting with his legs crisscrossed, *applesauce*, eyes closed, open palms resting on his knees, a smile filling his face. Oh, how she hated him then. The stories he told now, about what he could do. Had done.

And then she saw it with her own eyes—the boy so still, for so long, that a gimpy squirrel approached him, sniffing out the acorns he had placed in each open hand, its hind leg crooked, fur missing, a scar running across the mottled flesh. The little creature took first one acorn and then the other, chewing at the shell, getting to the meat, finally resting in the boy's lap, and—against all odds—taking a well-deserved nap. The boy stroked the animal, gently, his hands resting on its hindquarters, his face rippling in pain as if he'd found a tack, and not soft fur. Her blood boiled. She opened the door and shooed the creature away, its gait no longer hesitant or slow, bounding to the nearest tree and up it in a flash.

When the boy opened his eyes and turned to her, she scowled.

"Did you see?" he asked.

"No," she growled.

"You did. I know it."

"There is nothing special about you," she whispered, her dark side of the scale dipping lower, as his face shone brightly in the sun.

It had come to this.

The rest of the summer would find strange cars parked in the driveway, bikes tossed to the grass, neighbors wandering over to return borrowed power tools, each of them pausing to say hello to the boy. They made it a point to shake his hand, slowly, to grasp them both, to hold them a little bit longer than necessary. He knew. And he smiled. Sometimes they gave him a hug, and he would hug them back, fearless, hands on their shoulders, sometimes moving lower to where a kidney might reside. Eventually he set a basket on the edge of the porch, so the giving would be less awkward, the words needed to explain, to thank, to rejoice now left on quivering lips—this would be their secret as well. The basket filled with candy and toys, with crumpled-up dollar bills, jars of fruit preserves, and plates of homemade cookies—whatever they had to offer.

Robert was not blind to Rachel's descent, it had been up and down as long as he could remember, but there was so much darkness now, so much pain. He felt that he had driven her there with his joy, his love of life—and his gift.

He offered her a deal, but she refused. She hated him now. Perhaps it was too late. So he decided to trick her.

On the next full moon, when the parents were asleep, they went out to the back yard, behind the pile of wood for the winter, past the birdhouse swinging in the breeze from a rope tied to an ancient oak tree, past the pet cemetery down by the azaleas, to the makeshift altar the girl had built.

"What is it you want to see?" she'd said.

"Any of it," he whispered. "All of it."

She smiled in the darkness. She'd been building the shrine for days—the sticks, the feathers—the twine. There were acorn husks, a rotten apple, and a handful of writhing earthworms. There was paint in complicated hieroglyphics—stars, and circles, and lines. When she chewed at her ragged fingernail, pulling away a bit of keratin, blood blossomed to the surface, running down her finger, a single red coin landing on the rock below.

Robert acted quickly.

He took her hands, as she gasped and tried to escape, holding them tight, his own fingers now slick with her blood.

"You will not come undone," he said, anger flushing to the surface, a truth that danced across his skin, his eyes fading, his skin dulling. He pulled her close and held her tight. She struggled at first and then, realizing how strong he was, gave in. Her pain and suffering, it quieted for a moment, the voices dissipating, her tension unwinding into his frame. They met somewhere in the middle, brother and sister. A single cough, and the last of the glow escaped from his mouth, now a dancing firefly, heading out across the yard. As one lost its shine, the other filled with light, and as the moon overhead sat witness to it all, a shooting star ran across the sky, a spark of hope to all that saw it.

9.

FROM WITHIN

THE FIRST TIME THEY COME to measure my son, he is only eleven years old. Two men knock on the door of our humble home that squats on the outskirts of Shell County, my boy and I eating macaroni and cheese, our eyes turned mid-spoon to the interruption. Outside the darkness is as black as pitch, matching their uniforms, their helmets slick, a measuring tape in each of their hands, dust devils spinning across the land—dirt and garbage lifting high up into the night.

They never say a word, simply walk inside and lift the boy from his seat, one of them holding him as the other measures height, then width, then depth. They never speak, only nod at each other, and then retreat into the night, the door left open, as silt slips inside, and over the floor. I blink, the boy shrugs, and we go back to our meal. These things happen when your overlords float over the cities, some as small as cows, the queen bees as large as blimps. The smaller ones are gray, like elephants, the largest translucent—colored organs in red and purple pumping from within. They are beautiful and horrific, having ruined all we know.

I work in one of the mines, as most of us men do, out in the desert, certain ore that we previously thought of as common, essential to their life and continued development. Much like the storm troopers, I dress in a jumpsuit, but mine is orange, my son's a shade of peach. We do not reside in the gothic mansions that line the pit, no, we are just workers, so little to live for, but each other. And most days, that is enough. Our shotgun shacks ring out around the pillared homes, porches wrapping around the dirty gothic structures, foremen with shotguns, their women in tattered dresses.

The boy works in a sorting facility, an expansive metal garage on the way to the Shell County mines. At night we reunite on the dirt path outside his building, holding up our hands to reveal the day's labor—his lavender and blue from the kyanite, as if dusted by fairies; mine rusty and muted from carts of mica, splinters of the fine ore leaving nicks upon my skin. If it weren't for the boy, one arm around him as we lumber home, exhausted, I certainly would have ended it by now. All up and down my arms are thin lines of mottled flesh, spiderwebs of dark promises I can't keep—unable to leave, unable to surrender. He finds a way to chirp and laugh, something they discovered inside a mineral today, some sort of ancient bug—these buried worms and larvae, trapped inside the rock, the highlight of his day. He holds his hand out to show me the wriggling creatures, and my stomach turns over. They look prehistoric, with their pincers and feathered legs. I don't know if it's a beautiful thing, his discovery and excitement, or just another sad story in a long line of sad stories.

The second time they come to measure my son, I'm not nearly as receptive as the first. I ask them what they want, and why they are here; they simply push me aside and descend upon the boy. He is still so innocent, in this new world, never knowing the things I struggle to forget—free will, television, beer, football, movies, music, books, fine dining, travel—the list spirals out into the ether. He knows none of these pleasures, and never will. He stands up, his arms spread wide as they measure, and measure, and measure. I scream at them to get out, apoplectic with rage, my face flushing red, but they ignore me, simply nodding their heads—height, and width, and depth.

When I lay a hand on one of them, he turns on me with an unforeseen speed, a baton extending out of his hand, pulled from a pocket or his belt, perhaps, his gloved hand lined with metal spikes, the rapid-fire beating faster than I can witness, simply a blur of metal and blood splatter, my eyes, my nose, my teeth— my vision lost in a mist of red, as I fall to the ground, my hands never even raised.

When they are gone, and I regain consciousness, the boy is dabbing at my face with a bloody washcloth, the cold water calming my hot flesh, his eyes full of tears, his lips bit and puckered in resolve, never saying a word. He understands his place, and his eyes implore me to remember mine.

I do not miss any work; this is not allowed. So, beaten and bruised, I make my way to the mines. The boy splits off at his juncture in the path, releasing my hand with reluctance. We have learned not to ask, when somebody disappears—no longer standing next to us as we shovel, pick, and dig. We have learned to ignore the loss of fingers, the cuts and markings, changing in and out of our uniforms, backs covered in streaked lashings, weeping flesh, the whippings carried out in private, to keep us in constant fear. If the setting sun has no time of descent—no marked hour, or minute, or path—then how can we anticipate the darkness?

The third time they come, it is not to measure my boy but simply to take him. There are four guards this time, the first entering our filthy home with an electric cattle prod in front of him, pushing it into my raised hands, my strained chest, shock rippling over my flesh as I collapse to the floor, twitching while urine trickles down my shaking leg. And the boy never says a word as they extend their measuring tapes—height, and width, and depth. They nod to each other, jotting down a few notes, walking him out of the house as he tells me he loves me, tells me to be strong, to wait for him. They take him, leaving behind a small envelope with a few sentences about his new assignment. I do not know if he will return. He fits the mold for some strange new job, something about the health of the great ones, a bitter pill that the beasts must swallow—the medicine, somehow, my boy.

I know that I've taught him well, my son, even if I don't take my own advice. He has heard repeatedly that resistance is futile—my words slipping over his drooping eyes as he lies in bed, drifting off to sleep. I don't give him hope, when I tuck him in at night, because I can't give him something I don't have.

There are three great beasts that hover over our mine, their veiny skin transparent. I see them every day when I walk to work, and I hate their bluish tint, their waving tentacles, with all of my trembling heart. It's not like people haven't tried to rebel, to rise up. I've seen men rush out of the pits with rifles, blood on their hands, firing at the smaller gray ones, the great clear beasts in the sky rippling with puncture wounds. They pass right through them, holes made, certainly, but little changing. And as the smaller gray ones swarm closer, appendages descending, the men's screams are lost in the thick alien hides, ripped limb from limb as shots ring out, one or two of the elephantine creatures falling to Earth, more vulnerable it seems, the hovering mother-ships unharmed.

It's all I can think about in the weeks to come, my boy, and his new job. There are whispers from the other men, no women down here in the mines, their work elsewhere in the pleasure districts of Moosejaw. My wife was dead of cancer long before any of this horror fell upon us, and I thank whatever gods are left that she never had to witness this decay. The boy has her quiet optimism, so I trudge back and forth to the mines, lost in the dust and noise, waiting to hear something—anything at all.

There are whispers at work, quiet conversations slipped between the spark of the pickaxe, the rattling thunder of jack-hammers, sledges, and shovels down here close to the veins of ore. I sidle up to two men who are bagging up mica, as overhead and in the distance great excavators rumble past, bulldozers and graders spanning out across the dirt. They speak of their boys, measured and taken, and I ask what they know. They shake their heads and scatter like cockroaches, but before they separate I hear a few things. They are sick, the big ones, shedding scales of flesh that fall from the sky like graying snowflakes. I think of the sloughs of skin that have turned up over the past few weeks, great sheets of dry skin drifting about the dead land like tumbleweeds spinning in the wind. They hang lower in the sky, the men mumbled, and as I walk home from work, I scan the sky for confirmation. There are only two of them visible today—one as vibrant and glowing as ever; the second slightly lower, dull and hardly moving; the third one having fallen onto a distant mountain range, its sickly skin like a dirty blanket draped over pristine snow.

The final knock at my door is nothing I expect—the boy standing there skinny and sick, his eyes shrunken, his face sallow—falling into my outstretched arms. He says that up close they are magnificent creatures, so very large, the quiet inside the floating bodies like nothing he's ever witnessed. I take him to his bed, and set him down gently, fetching him a glass of water, his eyes electric with stories. He wants to tell me everything, so I sit on his bed and listen.

He talks of the other boys, how they were to be fed to the beasts, wrapped in protective coatings, slick jumpsuits made of glossy materials, treated with certain chemicals to aid their healing treatment. The boy laughs, coughing up phlegm and blood, his eyes glazing over as he tries to finish his tale. Holding his bony right hand, I listen, as he smiles a crimson smile. A simple job, he says, swimming their way to the center of the monsters, against the vibrating cilia. Not just medicine, which the creatures can't swallow, skin too thin to inject, too tough for any spray, but specific instructions about hearts and valves, chambers and ventricles, how to remove any blockages, plaque, or disease.

But they had another plan, he says, grinning, holding out his left fist. When he spreads his fingers wide, it is the worm again, now grown, ten times its previous size, pincers snapping, as big as a mouse, eyes blood-red, feathered legs twitching, wings now on its back, thin membranes lined with intricate patterns.

The boy is asleep now—his pulse slow, but steady. I take the worm, the caterpillar, whatever it is now, whatever it might become next—moth, or snake, or lizard—to the kitchen in search of a proper receptacle. I find a Mason jar and drop it inside, an iridescence rippling over its skin, feelers probing the air, as I poke a few holes in the lid with a rusty old screwdriver, my stomach rippling with hope.

I go to the front door and swing it open, the sky filled with orange light as the sun sets in the distance. They are gone; the sky is empty now—nothing hovering, a stream of men from the pits, gray-skinned husks lying scattered over the earth, the worms devouring from within. The sickness has spread, the network of creatures like one long line of electrostatic shock, stilling their waving arms as they wither and die across the silent barren plains, our new home.

10.

THE CAGED BIRD SINGS IN A DARKNESS OF ITS OWN CREATION

IN THE MOST NORTHERN REACHES of the Silverpine Forest, past the lumber mill, east of the abandoned mine, just this side of Devil's Gorge, there is a hut. It's nothing special, really, scraps of wood and sheet metal, held together with rumor and rusty nails, a roof made out of old billboards, a hint of a cereal ad peeking through, with a splash of red—a faded logo barely visible.

How is it still standing after all this time? That can be debated.

Perhaps it was built in the shadow of a huge oak tree that shades the structure, protecting it, the occasional acorns raining down on the wood-and-metal roof, creating a ripple of percussion in the otherwise quiet forest. Maybe it's the animal fat that is slathered over the frame, the sinew wrapped around one board after another, dried now, creating a bond, which might be cemented even further tomorrow, or the next day. Or it might be something else entirely—an illusion, some sort of glimmer of technology rippling under the building, a line of gold running through the tiny house, as if a motherboard had been pressed into the rotting wood, a surge of electricity running over it all, then fading as the sun pushes through the dense foliage. Whatever is happening here, the old man standing in the doorway holds a flickering presence, both daunting in the shadow and void he creates, but vulnerable in his sickly, thin appearance, an old flannel shirt barely covering his pale flesh and bony arms, dirty jeans leading down to black boots that are grotesquely oversized, the only bit of joy being his shockingly bright hair in a rainbow of colors, as well as a red bulbous nose in the center of his face. He grabs the sphere and rips it off, leaving behind a gap where a fleshy proboscis must have once resided, flinging the spongy crimson ball to the forest floor, where it bounces into a pile of leaves and disappears. He turns and heads back into the residence, the nose back on his face, a bit of magic here, the illusion continuing.

When the acorns fall again, he begins weeping, muttering the name of a long-lost love under his breath, his sobs turning into a rasping cough, then to something darker—something wet. Other random noises emanate from the hut—sometimes from him, and sometimes from the dozens of jars that line the walls, shelves full of clear glass, and a curiosity of items. As he rolls about on the cot, transferring white paste and powder to the dirty sheets and blankets, the tension in his stomach builds until he leans over and vomits up a long stream of tangled balloons, in a shocking mix of rubber iridescence. Mixed in with the puddle of primary colors is a smattering of glitter, a few chunks of some glistening meat, some sawdust, and a handful of marbles that go rolling across the floor.

In the jars, there is much more. A tiny heart floats in a yellowing liquid, somehow still beating. Next to it, a bowl filled with yo-yos, the strings dirty, crusted with brown stains, a meaty smell lifting off of the faded toys. A large glass Mason jar holds nothing but hair—long blond strands, several puffs of dark, curly tightness, and brown clippings in a number of lengths, all mixed together.

It doesn't stop there.

A little glass music box is filled with glittering metal—rings, and necklaces in silver and gold, some plastic, some onyx, all inlaid with memory, and trace amounts of DNA. Next to that is a large clear vase filled with toothbrushes in a variety of colors—some brand-new, or nearly that, others worn down, the bristles frayed, handles bent and faded, the edges worn away from use. There is a jar filled with flickering fireflies, humming and buzzing in the night. A clay bowl is overflowing with little rubber balls that mix and mingle, vibrating with hate and sorrow. A gilded cage toward the back of the little room is filled to bursting with tiny birds, in a cacophony of pigmentation—chirping red, twittering blue, gasping black into the encroaching night. There is so much pain gathered here, and the sobbing form lying on the floor knows exactly what he's done, the role he has played in all this sadness.

As the darkness settles in around the humble abode, the hut goes quiet, a crinkling of leaves buried under snapping sticks, the tall shadows outside standing in a semicircle around the building, their long necks and slender arms extending in ways that are hard to rationalize. Six of these elongated figures hold court in this desolate forest, chittering to each other, a dull glow seeping from their myriad eyes. Their skeletal frames rise nearly to the top of the encroaching trees, their oval heads brushing up against the green leaves, bent over in worship, or perhaps just to get a closer look.

Inside, he stirs, swallows with some effort, a coil of madness unfurling in his gut, the time for his departure at hand. He has played host for so many years now, as a series of black-and-white photos unfurls in front of his watering eyes: cracking jokes in grade school, sent to the corner of the room, a dunce cap on top of his head; sitting at a bar sipping beer and telling stories as the women eased in closer, the laughter slipping from their blushed lips, their eyes crinkling with happiness; the television cameras bearing down on his face as he cavorted for their amusement, the children at his feet filled with wonder, the ache in his gut swirling around and around.

He knows they are here now, returned. But the price he had to pay, it seems exorbitant, out of balance with what he has reaped, what has been sowed. In the beginning, there was no length he wouldn't go to in order to get back what he loved. But, over time, the cost grew and expanded, one more task, one more item, until there was no turning back.

In for a penny, in for a pound.

And that pound of flesh has been taken. Over and over again.

To what end?

Eventually it was inverted. Not the death of one for the good of many, but the opposite—the death of many for the good of one. Or the few.

Or so he thought.

As the ripples of his actions scattered across the globe, and beyond, the man with the funny shoes and the yellowing eyes wept into his trembling hands. And the worm in his belly squirmed with a heady anticipation.

They were going home.

• • •

Somewhere in the dark, millions of miles away, and yet entirely on top of this event, so very distant, and essentially filling the same space, a massive pair of hands is busy creating. They are moving quickly—a blur—but, upon closer inspection, moving infinitely slow. There is a vast tableau in front of this being, spilling out in every direction, the great presence surrounded by satellites of life, motes of dark energy, electric fields riddled with animation—so many sights, sounds, and smells.

Taking a deep breath in, it exhales into its fists, a flurry of feathers circling like a fixed tornado in blue and white, spinning around and around, forming a murmuration of life and movement. Off to the left, several hundred bluebirds scatter into the never-ending darkness.

The hands reach out into the ether and conjure up a handful of dirt, packing it in tightly, then reaching up as if to find a lost memory, pulling twigs and berries out of nothingness, pushing the wood and red juice together, tugging here and there, eventually opening its massive hands to spill out a herd of deer, some antlers budding, others fully formed, the creatures standing on wobbly legs, then dashing off in excitement and fear.

Holding one giant hand over the other, its fingertips sprinkle dust and droplets of water over the cupped hand below, and a squirming starts to spool and twist in the palm of the mighty being—dark green, the smell of algae and seaweed swimming up into the air, one tentacle after another pushing out of the mass, growing faster and faster until it overflows the hand that holds it. With a sigh and a squinting eye, the beast shoves a handful of sharp teeth into the wriggling creature, an undulating mass of tiny bulbous eyes crammed into the middle of the rippling mass. When it surges again, it is released into the darkness, a singular monstrosity, destined for a distant planet, an ocean with unlimited depths.

This has been happening for a long time, it is happening now, it will happen for all of eternity.

The maker bends over and snaps its fingers, lighting a fire at its fingertips, the flames licking at what must be flesh, trying to cajole the flickering light, a difficult task, the smell of meat cooking, an earthy wood burning sweet and smoky, the sinuous form leaping out of the gesticulating hands before it is complete, before it becomes what was planned. But this is life, this is creation—intention, and then chaos.

With a long, steady blow, a wind leaves its massive lips, a funnel of cool air whirling about in the space before it, swirling and taking on mass—long, leathery wings extending—the creator narrowing its gaze, shaking its head, trying to manipulate the shape, as a beak elongates and talons scratch at the air, first one winged beast, then two, doubling in number, released with frustration, scales and needles spilling behind them, this experiment another failure.

Only two, it thinks. It could have been worse.

And in its anger it makes a fist, pounding what would have been a table, a surface, if such things existed here, but it finds resistance nonetheless. And in that singular gesture, a spark of atoms spills out of the clenched fingers, a sickly yellow cancer spreading out and over the trembling knot of digits, the tiny flashes of light and oozing sickness taking on a microscopic form, expanding and then contracting, breeding in and of itself; and when its presence is noticed, fully formed, it disappears into the ether, death wandering out to claim its stake—seeking out weakness, and feeding on misery.

It pauses for a moment, this rippling being, taking in a deep breath, its many forms shifting as a wave of emotions washes over it. Calm, collected, legs folded, hand on knees. Then its head tilts back, its eyes ablaze, as a deep laughter builds up from inside tainted flesh, feet to hooves, and then nubs bursting from a cracking skull. It inhales, and its pale flesh expands, running a hand over its bald head, an expanding belly, a gleam in its eyes, a smile upon its fleshy face. And then its arms double, then triple, a third eye upon its forehead, a glitter of gold sprinkling down like rain from a cloud, a clash of symbols, and then silence.

It was all things, it is all things, it will be all things.

It goes back to work.

It focuses for a moment on humankind—and pulling a sack of what might be seen as marbles out of the darkness, it spills the assortment of spirits upon a false ground. In a flurry of activity, the shapes ping off each other—a clacking sound, and then a great sigh, a moan of contentment, and then a cry of fear and loss, as it manipulates the dozens of entities with a deft touch and a sharp eye. They shiver into life. A push here, a pinch there, a whisper to this handful, cupped up close to its mouth, and then scattered back on the floor, a sparking of blue and green, and a flash of red and orange, a singular white orb spinning and hovering all by itself, while a solitary black sphere sits in one place, vibrating with anger and vengeance.

It scatters the bulk of these new beings out into the universe, some seeking light, others wallowing in the endless darkness. It picks up the only one left, the obsidian globule, bringing it close to its trembling eyes, the hard shell cold in its grip, a shallow pulse of warm light buried within, that sparks white, sparks yellow, flashes a momentary glow that makes its creator smile.

It is given a name now; it is shown how to bring joy to the world, the children; it is told of how other life might exist far beyond its reach; and the creator warns of how such power and knowledge might corrupt, eventually.

And then it is set free.

It is born unto the earth.

It will hear laughter in the form of innocent children.

And it will make decisions—both horrible and inspired.

Such is life.

• • •

At a very young age, Edward Carnby had the first in a series of visions that would transform and define his life. And because he believed what he saw, these moments had great power—to alter his future, and those futures of the people around him as well.

Some say that the tall shadows were nothing more than a fever, a flu when he was lost in the woods, a sickness that caused the boy to lie in bed for weeks on end, a cancer in his bones that would cause a slight limp in his gait. Others can confirm what was there in the forest—too many concrete details kept in their fluttering minds, in metal cans at the back of closets, in safe deposit boxes, the keys rusty and lost long ago. There is no real way to explain away the tiny knobs, levers, and bits of heavy black rock that was melted into odd shapes. Found downstream, in the back of caves, and buried deep in an assortment of fields—the materials they were made of cannot be found anywhere on Earth.

But there may be a third explanation here as well.

Three moments, three wishes.

What happened?

At the age of twelve, Eddie used to wander the woods in search of arrowheads, empty wasp nests, tree bark curled into sheets of paper, and bright blue robins' eggs—some intact, others cracked open, and empty. He was fascinated by the offerings nature presented to him. He might find a field filled with budding flowers—in yellow and purple, with hints of red. He might see in the ponds, lakes, and creeks a variety of silver-backed fish swimming in schools, some with a wash of shimmer and a stripe of color—perch, trout, bass, and carp. And sometimes he found death—that egg cracked open with a bit of fluff and bone inside, a single eye gazing up; a skeleton riddled with a sour stench inside a thorny bush, the red of its fur faded and damp; now and then just a splash of blood, and a bit of sinew, nothing left but a stain, with buzzing flies marking the expiration.

It all fascinated him—life, death, and everything in between.

It was on one of these hikes that he found the shadow child, a thin trail of smoke leading up into the sky, a dent in the earth, and a smattering of flickering metal across a field of puffing dandelions. There was an echo in his head, his ears filled with the sound of cascading water, and at the same time it was entirely quiet.

When a baby bird falls from a nest, the story is that it shouldn't be touched, that any kind of interaction with human flesh will taint the creature, the mother bird pecking it to death, sensing only trouble and danger. This is not true. But that doesn't mean the action goes unnoticed, that the bird is not aware, that the gesture is not recorded—for future action, good or bad.

Of course Eddie bent over and touched the clear gel, the shadow pulsing within it, the strange form lying prostrate in the dirt, a hum of some machine winding down, the smell of oil and plastic burning. It was unlike anything he had ever seen.

He thought there were words slipping from the form, some sort of plea. As he knelt in the field, in the itching grass and moist soil next to the fading silhouette, it was in his nature to touch it, his hand slipping through the glistening form, a gasp from them both, a ringing of bells, a stinging across his flesh, a triggering of some alarm, his body suddenly covered in a sheen of sweat. It was electric, it was liquid, it was a marking in self-defense by the creature lying beneath him.

He pulled his hand back, and the shadow dissipated, the remaining gelatinous shape seeping into the earth, Eddie's hand held up high in front of his flickering gaze—glowing red, then absorbing into his flesh, around him the metal and plastic smoking, melting—reduced to ash, the wind scattering the detritus to the far corners of the field.

Standing up, it was all gone. No smoke, no fragments or evidence—just an empty field, the sound of wildlife slipping back into focus. The boy swallowed hard and turned in a circle. He walked the field, pushing aside long grass, sending dandelion seeds flying, but nothing more. He was unable to see the remnants, his vision distorted forever, altered in some crucial ways. It would be much later when others would find the strange remains.

He looked to the sky, asking for an explanation, wishing for something more. He was eager to learn, to grow, to comprehend.

That would be a mistake.

Later that night, he would take a very long time to fall asleep.

The next day, the memory would fade, and he would forget it had ever happened.

Mostly.

Almost.

But not quite.

It would be twelve years down the road, at the ripe old age of twenty-four, that he would revisit this moment, in an entirely different way.

Standing in an alleyway outside a local bar, smoking a cigarette and thinking about a girl who was inside playing pool, Eddie noticed a gathering of shadows down by the trash cans and dumpsters. For a moment he thought it was some local boys he'd had trouble with in the past—simple folk who had no aspirations, often offended by his lengthy conversations, the attention of blondes and brunettes alike stirring up something close to a primal, territorial rage. But it wasn't those kids.

In an instant, Eddie was on his knees, one hand held up, inspected by the shifting shadows, a glow spilling into the night. His mouth opened as if to scream, but nothing came out. His vision was watery, *shimmering*, a darkness descending upon him like a ratty blanket, the smell of smoke and burning plastic filling the air, and, before he passed out, a sharp pain in his gut. They would hardly leave a mark. The only evidence of this moment was a tiny red dot—something a mosquito, or spider, might make.

When he wakes, there is only one thought in his head.

Wait.

Don't go.

Hold on.

It is fading fast, the memory, but he has glimpsed something extraordinary, and he wants to see more.

And he will. In time.

In the coming weeks, he will get sick—a fever of 103; a horrible rash that creeps across his skin in mottled hues; nausea that causes him to vomit into the toilet with a violent upheaval, the blood and mucus dotted with tiny flecks of metal, all triggering some deeper knowledge that he is afraid to truly recognize.

And then it is gone.

The hosting is complete.

His work is only beginning.

The third time will cement their relationship, ten years later, as he sits in front of a mirror, putting on his makeup, the lights on the dressing table bright yellow, a smile splitting his face, as he glues on the red nose, pulls the wig on tight, a wriggle of anxiety in his gut.

There is a woman, Gina.

She is everything he has ever wanted in a woman—long blond hair, glimmering blue eyes, curves hidden beneath modest dresses, and an easy smile that fills his gut with mating butterflies.

For Edward, this is the love of his life, a relationship that has bloomed over the last couple of years, through cups of coffee, dancing at local watering holes, seeing her out in the audience at his shows, smiling with glee.

For Gina, these are merely coincidences, a Venti Mocha on the way to work with a nod to the strange pudgy man in the corner booth, a night out with the girls at the only place to dance in miles, a visit to the television station to laugh at the clown, a bit of a local celebrity, kept at a safe distance, after all.

In the shadows of his closet, there is a murmuring, a beckoning, and Edward, soon to be Krinkles (and *only* Krinkles) answers. He stands in the back of the tiny space and nods his head. He listens to what is offered. And it is set in motion.

It will spill out into the future.

Look close and see what it becomes.

See what you want to see, as Krinkles does.

The truth is a slippery fish.

• • •

When the tired old man leaves the hut once again, they are waiting. Patient for so long. With all their technology, their abilities, and their desire, they cannot walk the Earth in shadow, for the eyes of the planet are upon them. They have been seen, and they have been hurt.

But their work here is done now.

And in a blink, they vanish.

In a distant laboratory, the worm is removed under bright lights in a sterile environment. It is placed into a container where later it will be downloaded, dissected, and documented for the benefit of them all.

In the living room of a quaint little cottage, just on the edge of an entirely different set of woods—not far from a rippling stream filled with colorful fish, and a field overflowing with blooming flowers and dancing grass—Edward sits and smiles. He rocks in his chair, sipping a cup of chamomile tea, comfortable in his soft new flannel shirt, his faded jeans, the windows open, birdsong slipping in, the television quietly playing black-and-white shows from his childhood.

He laughs.

When the woman enters the room, he takes the plate with the ham-and-cheese sandwich on rye, a bit of Dijon mustard slathered on there, rippled potato chips, and a dill pickle on the side. She kisses his forehead, and he thanks her, saying her name. It's a recognizable name. When she enters the kitchen, her skin flickers, the tapestry that is tightly wrapped over her metal frame, plastic shell, and colored wiring dissipating for a moment.

On a wall to the left of Edward is a large mirror. There are days he stares at it, thinking he sees a shimmer. But most of the time he is content. He thinks of his childhood, his career, the woman he loves, and while parts of it feel thin at times—a head-ache forming if he looks at it too closely—he is grateful.

Behind that mirror, there may only be a wall.

Behind that mirror, there might be men watching Edward, taking notes, and nodding their heads, smiling in the darkness, their work a success.

Behind that mirror, there could be elongated shadows, stretching to the ceiling, hunched over, chirping in the gloom, eyes glowing.

There may not be a mirror at all.

Edward may lie dying in that first forest, his dark deeds finally absorbing the last of his humanity, death a welcome respite.

The jars, the bowls, the DNA—perhaps they were stolen in secret, nobody harmed (especially not the children), saving an alien race from a plethora of sickness and disease.

Or maybe it's something much worse.

In the expanding corners of a never-ending universe, the creator smiles. Its work here is done.

II.

IN HIS HOUSE

Hello, my friend,

Thank you for taking the time to read my missive. I'm not sure exactly where this has ended up. I've been sending out this note for millennia now, in so many forms. Perhaps you are reading this someplace in public—tacked up in a grocery store or taped to a telephone pole. Maybe this arrived in your mailbox in the form of a letter. I've even heard that it has somehow worked its way into various collections of fiction, passing itself off as a story. How amusing. However it got to you, thank you for taking the time to read it. My fractured soul depends on your help here, your involvement, your support.

ph'nglui mglw'nafh Cthulhu R'lyeh wgah'nagl fhtagn

Don't worry about how you pronounced it; you saw it with your mind, the letters were arranged and presented. That is all that matters here.

That wasn't so painful now, was it?

Keep reading.

Thank you.

I have lived in the shadows for so long now, trying to rid myself of this unholy curse. It has not been easy. But what I've found is that humanity is not without heart. I'm counting on that, my friend, your kindness here, and your willingness to keep reading. You'd be surprised at how few stop . . . even when presented with such strange, hard-to-pronounce words. No, people keep reading. Especially if they feel as if they can help somebody, if somebody is in distress.

Human nature, I suppose.

I can remember seeing so many examples of this over the years, and it has always given me hope. And that is what I needed, to find not just a handful of willing supplicants, I mean, *kind citizens*, to take a tiny bit of this weight off my shoulders, by the hundreds, no, thousands. You are one of many. You are legion.

I've seen women tied to stakes, and the flames lit, only to have an uprising mount, rebellion in the form of pitchforks and dull knives—justice dispensed. I've seen men strung up with rope for the color of their skin, the threads cut before the trapdoor opened its gaping maw, the innocent falling through, and running away—free at last, the crowd in hushed anger, smiles creeping over so many, many faces. I've seen cars plummet into ponds, lakes, rivers, off bridges—Good Samaritans risking their own lives to dive into the water and pull out the driver—no matter the details—mouth covered with tape, hands tied, teeth knocked out, buck naked. Always presumed innocent.

So rarely true.

And I sense you listening now, taking this all in. Curious. Wondering how you got here and what you might be able to do, how you can help.

It's not hard.

I just need you to listen.

And keep listening.

That part is essential.

I need you to recite a few strange words into the morning sun, or the afternoon doldrums, or the long, ever-expanding night. Wherever you are, whenever you are, whoever you are.

In his house, he waits dreaming.

I had dreams once of a life filled with laughter and love, friendship and success, so many ways that my innocent childhood might unfurl into adult responsibilities, and fulfillment.

None came to pass.

Instead, I live in the shadows now, in the gaps between the letters, the very letters you are reading right now, my friend.

ph'nglui mglw'nafh Cthulhu R'lyeh wgah'nagl fhtagn

That's twice now. Good, good . . . we're getting somewhere. Don't give up now; don't turn away. I know you want to see how this turns out . . . what you've gotten yourself into. That cat is so curious, right?

Silly cat.

We don't have that far to go now; just relax, and this will all be over soon. But maybe I can at least help explain how you got here and what brought us together. Yes?

I think so.

It's the least I can do.

You've been feeling unhappy of late, right? Correct? Not satisfied with the way things are going. There has been a sadness at the periphery, black motes when you close your eyes, rubbing your eyelids with your fingers, fireworks buried under the flesh. Something looming . . . perhaps a sense of dread? Anxiety worming its way over your flesh, a sheen of sweat dotting your brow, your upper lip shining in the dark. You've been saying prayers at night, my friend, lying on your back, staring at the ceiling.

"Why me?" you say.

"Why *not* me?" you ask. "I deserve better. I deserve more."

Yes, you do.

We all want to live deliciously.

Nobody wants to be a footnote.

When you are awake at night, unable to sleep, and you open your mind, heart, and soul to the universe, you should probably be more specific. There are many gods, and many lords. You have not framed your requests in the appropriate Latin phrases; you have not quoted from texts that are clear and concise. You have been broad in your desperation.

In your urgency, you have opened the windows, flung wide the door, and shouted to the darkest corners of the universe that you are an endless void, a bottomless pit, seeking something greater to fill you up with light.

Without light, there cannot be shadow.

Without shadow, we cannot exist.

I sense in your daily life there has been a burning, a building up of something grand, waiting for release. You are no longer patient. You are frustrated. You see the world around you drowning in chaos, and you wonder why these things are allowed to happen.

It is a numbing, a beating-down, a litany of broken promises, dark words uttered in the night, to lost souls who have nowhere else to go. If they were to truly search these lies and distractions, they would know it was all false.

But they do not seek the truth.

Not really.

They only seek privilege.

They only want to be in the majority.

To have the world the way that best serves them, and only them.

It is an extremely narrow way of viewing it all.

And it will be their downfall.

Even now, I see you are starting to question this. But I'm afraid it's too late. You are too far gone now. I could tell you to step away, but you won't. You are standing there, sitting there, lying there—reading these words—and yet you will not put this calling down. You will not turn away. There is a hint that something amazing might happen, that you have discovered something truly spectacular. That you have been chosen.

And you're not wrong.

You *have* been chosen.

As I once was, so very long ago.

But I have grown tired, and promises were made.

I just had to be clever, look between, recruit, rephrase, rejoice.

I would like to talk to you about our Lord and Savior—The High Priest of the Great Old Ones, The Eternal Dreamer, The Sleeper of R'lyeh.

He will be your undoing.

He will remake you in his image.

As he has done with me.

In the shadows, I have seen humankind push itself to the very brink of annihilation, only to pull itself back, time and time again. But we are so close now. Perhaps you are the linchpin, the impetus, the catalyst for change that we need so urgently.

You have a chance to go down in history here, to be one of the many that led to the great awakening.

Dig deep, really ask yourself what it is that is so important. What are you doing? What have you done?

My friend, you can live forever.

We are all matter, tiny atoms, held together by so very little. Become one with us, become something greater.

In the beginning, I, too, questioned it all, my place in the pantheon, my role in the great undoing. And when I released my ego, when I let go of my humanity, I saw how things might be—the expanding darkness, the eternity, the peace. How it might right the scales and silence the masses.

It is time to wipe the slate clean, to start over, the God of Light given his chance, his time—the Lord of Darkness ready to reign. An eye for an eye, a tooth for a tooth.

In the coming plague, all will be sorted, and none will be denied. The liars will be told the truth and shown the errors of their ways. The bigots will be rightly educated—for all of mankind is the same—born into sin, a slow descent into madness and betrayal. The rapists and murderers will be torn asunder—one agonizing digit and limb at a time, shown the many ways that they may suffer, too, and it will be glorious, their undoing.

You will not be alone.

There was a time in the beginning when I too questioned the plan—staring out over the deadlands, the wastelands, at the dry desert landscape, the hellfires that burned over the horizon, the masses growing in number, filling in one valley after another. The way the earth cracked open, strange appendages and tentacles spooling out of the steaming cracks. The forests at the edge of the mountains spilling creatures on four legs, humping and galloping over the foliage, and into the high grasses as the growth turned into spoil. And up over the range lurked flying beasts with cracked, leathery wings—thick purple veins running through the expanding, unfurling flesh—elongated skulls holding back rows of sharp teeth, chittering in the settling gloom. Below the hills, pools of water, sometimes blue, but more likely a mossy green, a dark scum, filled with gelatinous blobs, covered with spiky hairs, a collection of yellowing eyes atop what might have been considered some kind of head. And snapping at my own heels, the furry creatures with mottled, diseased skin revealed in chunks, snouts exposed to show the fractured, bony skulls beneath it all, long, slavering tongues distending, lapping at the foul air around us.

Yes, I paused.

I wondered.

As you may be wondering now.

What have you done, exactly, here?

And how can you undo it now?

ph'nglui mglw'nafh Cthulhu R'lyeh wgah'nagl fhtagn

The third time, thrice it has been uttered.

It is too late now, my friend.

You are one of us now.

There is no point in tossing the book across the room, in tearing the letter to shreds, in crumpling up the post, or in deleting the email that somehow ended up infecting your computer. What has been done is now done.

There will come a time, in the not-so-distant future, when you will be summoned. The call cannot be ignored. It will ring true, deep into the night, so prepare yourself for the looming war, the encroaching darkness, and know that you have chosen well.

It was always going to be this way, so take your seat among the minions burbling at the feet of our master, and do his bidding, as you've always been destined to do.

When you closed your eyes and cried out into the darkness, you asked for help. It has arrived. When you said, "Anyone, any-where, please...," know that you were heard, and that your long-ing will soon be satiated. You do not have to worry any longer; take a deep breath, my friend, and surrender to the darkness.

As I once did.

As I continue to do.

But not for long.

You, and millions like you, have diverted his attention away from me, bit by bit, step by step, piece by piece. And when his gaze finally shifts to the growing army that lingers at the foot of the mountains, at the edge of the great forest, by the cracked earth and undulating waters, I will be free. You have a role now, a job to do, and in it you will be fulfilled, made whole—in your greed, and selfishness, and whining impatience.

My work here is done.

The Great Dreamer awakens.

In his house, there will be much suffering.

12.

OPEN WATERS

THE FIRST SENSATION I feel when I come to is a thrumming in my legs, so I must be alive. The room is quiet, the world outside this tiny hut a blanket of silence; my ears strain to find life. A wave of swelling rolls over my body, my hands aching, as a dull throb at the back of my head pulses on. Nothing has changed. It is now as it always was—eternal damnation.

Lying in the small bed, I sit up, eyes blurry and red, stinging, a long breath taken in and a longer one let out. I cannot walk yet—it's better if I simply lie back down. I always wake up broken, and weak, as if tired from a long journey, my soul slipping back into its frame. It takes time for the small house to come back into focus, for my body to feel the thin mattress, for my eyes to adjust to the shifting colors and landscape around me. Sometimes the palette is warm, and sometimes it is cold; but if I close my eyes and breathe in deeply, it resets, and slides back into focus. I'm used to it—to the anomalies I find on a daily basis.

I can no longer differentiate between waking life and my dreams. Too many times I have woken up in the long grass, or at the edge of the cliffs, or even in the dampness of the caves to the west. I wander. I chew on the red leaves that I find scattered at the base of the mammoth tree that holds court in the south. I run from the wolves. Things have shifted and changed, even in my time here, after the floods, long after the disease took Isabella, my love. And yet I have not aged.

There is a boat down on the white sands at the east side of the island. It has also been here for as long as I can remember. I do not have a compass, I have not been able to build one either, so the times I spend rowing out into the ocean, they are essentially slow attempts at suicide. The water is too deep, of course, to leave a marker, to push a stick down into the murky depths, or even to drop anchor—far too deep for that to work. There may be other ways to mark my passing, to chart these expeditions, but I haven't figured them out yet. I push out into the endless black yawn and head in one direction as best as I can. My shoulders strain, a heat spreading across my back, a thousand needles embedded in my biceps, until the island is almost gone from sight. It is at that moment when the panic finally washes over me, that I stop rowing and drift—eyes glued to the island, slowly drifting, a wind picking up and spraying me with a fine, salty mist. It is then that I dare to turn my head. In every direction, I stare as far as I can, my eyes tracking the slow roll of the dark waters out to my left, out to my right, the boat tipping as I turn all the way around. I see shadows rolling underneath the hull, but they never reveal themselves to me. Sometimes it is one large, black presence; other times it is a school of three. But they never break the surface.

And then nothing. The silence is deafening. So I turn the boat around in a lazy circle and head back to the white shores that are my home.

There is no need to glance over my shoulder as I turn back, as I cover the same distance that I'd just unfurled, coiling the imaginary line back in, reeling the boat into the island once again. Overhead, a gray gull swoops low, its long beak opening, scooping, a wriggling fish caught in its mouth, the fish holding a long black-and-orange-striped snake, the serpent biting down on a quiet cricket. I feel my stomach gurgle with hunger. I can't remember the last time I really ate a meal. Soon enough the shallow waters push up to the boat, and I coast into the shore. The island always pulls me back, no matter how I row.

I've set out in every direction imaginable, from the beaches, from the base of the caves, from the bottom of the rocky cliffs. I mark my bearings, eyes set on one clump of sand, or one sprout of thorny grass high up on the rocks, and I row. In the beginning, it was just a way to pass the time, to tell myself that I had tried to escape, to find another island perhaps, other people, possibly a passing liner or ship. It was just a compulsive need to cross off squares on an imaginary map—north and then south, east and then west, an angle split between them, a diagonal off to a horizon that I could never find.

It did me no good.

One day in a fit of anger and drunk on potato vodka, I row in a single direction deep into the night. I laugh under the moon, howling out my rage, the darkness around me as if I had been submerged in a jar, dropped into an aquarium, loaded into a rusty van, and driven into an airplane hangar—a rolling sheet of glass, reflections of light, the rocking of the road and a series of abrupt potholes, engulfed by a giant metal frame. I slip out of my head and into the black pitch, cackling as my hands blister, smear, and bleed—the sweat pouring over my skin, dried into a salty grain, and then melted down to a liquid once again. When the sun comes up, there is nothing in sight, nothing to reward my manic departure. Before I can turn around to check my destination, the boat runs up on the dull white sand of the beach.

Home—there is no escaping it, this long, slow death.

•••

At the hut, I notice for the first time a light switch in the wall. On an island with no electricity or running water, it makes no sense. So I ease over to it, flick it up, and the world breaks.

I sit up in my apartment in Chicago and remove the virtual-reality goggles, rubbing my eyes as I take a deep breath. Through the faded, torn blinds, I see that the sky outside is gray and overcast, pollution keeping the haze in a perpetual state, the old windows rattling in their frames. The radiator clicks and hums, a dull heat emanating from its coiled form. There is a faint smell of urine, and mold, and as I go to stand up I feel a pinch in my right arm, as well as in my cock.

How long was I under?

I look up to the IV bag hanging on a single hook embedded in the wall and remove the needle from my arm. Lying on the ground next to my mattress is another bag, this one full, and leaking slightly, so I grimace and gently pull the catheter out of my shriveled flesh, the image of a mouse hidden in a small nest coming to mind. I grin, chuckle to myself, and then cough.

I see four metal water bowls lined up against the wall, all empty.

Shit.

Next to them is a giant bag of generic dry cat food, tipped over, food still spilling out onto the floor.

So she's not dead, I think. That's a bonus.

I hear a slurping sound coming from the bathroom and then the clicking of tiny nails on the hardwood floors. My gray-and-white cat, Isabella, wanders into the room, eyes squinting, as she scans the space, glaring at me, slowing down to sit on her haunches, judgment emanating from every ounce of her thin frame.

"I know," I say.

She blinks, licks a paw, runs it over her head, past her ears a few times, and stops. She inhales, as if considering her options, exhales, and forgives me, hopping onto the bed, snuggling into my lap. I don't deserve any of this. I'd fight back the tears if it made any difference, so, instead, I let them flow.

An alarm clock clicks into song, something about a final countdown, and I realize it's Monday morning, my vacation over. I hit the snooze button and pet my cat for a few moments, and then painfully work my way to the shower, where I soak until the hot water runs out. There is a bliss in the steam, a tiny bar of soap holding sandalwood and patchouli, a small pleasure in a world gone to hell.

I have a van to catch. My decision to join the Work Force, always something I reconsider when I stand in the cold, the sidewalk filled with young men and women—beards and ponytails, white skin and brown—all huddled together to combat the wind, few smiles to be found. There aren't many options left these days. Those at the top hiding out in their ivory towers, the rest of us down in the streets scratching and fighting over whatever stale scraps of bread are left.

When the white van pulls up, we all jostle closer, trying to stand out as virile, but not desperate, the faces now filled with a glow that can only be described as longing. I see the same people every time, until one day there is a void—the tall skinny Black kid with the afro, gone; the thick girl with the shaved head, and piercings in her eyebrow, missing; the twin boys in matching black hoodies with startling blue eyes, ghosts now. There is so little good news these days; we make the best of it where we can.

I am selected and climb in. Anyone over six feet tall tends to get pulled, and I am a few inches beyond that, though my pale skin works against me. As I nod to the burly, bald man with the clipboard, he squints and nods back, motioning me in.

"Steve," he mutters under his breath.

The stubble on his face is permanent, the stump of a cigar in one corner of his crooked mouth. I turn my gaze away before I say or do something stupid and screw up my work for the day. We don't have a great reputation, us Caucasians, often lazy and entitled, where the darker flesh is known for their hard work and reliability. I say a silent prayer to whatever gods are left roaming this fractured planet.

The week flies by in a blur of manual labor. Monday I paint houses on the south side of Chicago, everything white, trying to cover up the mold, seal the wood in tight from the airborne waste and disease. Tuesday it's cleaning up a burnt movie theater, rows of seats with the padding melted away—the smell of smoke staying on me for several days. Wednesday it's a suicide—the kitchen walls covered in dull colors and matter, the smell a sickly sweet wave of particles, bits of bone and flesh in every corner of the room—in coffee mugs, the toaster, across the stove, in pans and bowls. Thursday I am deep in the bowels of a new low-income housing high-rise just down the road from where I live, taking core soil samples out of the cold, wet earth, trying to show that the ground is stable enough to build on, I think. (It's not.) And Friday it's a long trip out to a coal barge where the Chicago River meets Lake Michigan. I spend all day lugging hundred-pound sacks of the dwindling resource back to a lab, where it'll be processed, tested, and checked for impurities. It all seems futile, but it passes the time.

Later in the evening, I undress and toss my clothes in the pile that has been slowly growing in the corner of my bedroom—hairballs and fur rolling across the floor like tumbleweeds—my own sour flesh and fluids causing my nose to wrinkle in disgust.

I pick up the game box off the kitchen counter and turn it over in my hands.

Open Waters.

I read the description on the back—hardly any information at all. I vaguely remember entering some data when I first bought it—favorite foods, childhood memories, my name and a physical description, things I owned and cherished.

I shrug and hop into the shower.

When I come out, the kitchen window is open, the sheer drapes billowing in a cold breeze, and I don't see the cat anywhere, a stiff mouse left on the windowsill—threat, or gesture of love, I'm not sure. She'll be back. A dusting of snow leaks into the room, the slamming of car doors outside echoing my own jittery heartbeat. I rustle through the cabinets and find half a pouch of dusty catnip. I scatter it on the floor, and by her scratching post, hoping the offering will buy me some favor.

It doesn't take long to fill the bowls with water, hook up a new IV, and ease the catheter back into my flesh. I only plan on staying for the weekend, but the last time that turned into ten days.

Nobody missed me at the curb outside; nobody missed me anywhere else. The new world order echoes with apathy. And I'm one of the voices in the chorus.

• • •

I sit up in the hut, rub the sleep out of my eyes, and smile. I pay attention today, and the things I find fill me with wonder. On the simple wooden table in the center of the hut, there is a metal bowl, and in it is a pile of watches—all of them with brown leather straps, in various states of wear and use, a silver case holding a white face with Roman numerals. It looks very familiar. There must be fifteen here. I find one that looks like it has been broken in, and I slip it on my left wrist, covering a trio of scars. It fits like a glove.

Next to it is a stack of manila paper, and several sharpened #2 pencils. I sit down in the requisite wooden chair and start drawing like I've never seen such items before. I run a line across the page, to create the horizon, and then sketch out tunnels down into the earth. I grin in the dim morning hours as the sun slowly rises outside the windows, pushing a rose-colored lens over the pane. In the tunnels, I add all kinds of danger—jagged blades and teeth, pits to fall into, doors that might open and close, upside-down bats, coiled serpents battling snakes, and at the end, in a bulbous room, a spider with twelve legs and a jittering mandible, perched in its web, a treasure chest under the looming form. For a moment I am filled with innocence, memories buried beneath the surface.

I stand and stretch, twisting my body into different positions, holding the forms, bending and pausing, distant languages whispering through my skull, a whiff of incense, all gone when I open my eyes. My back feels better, my spine no longer tight.

I head north today, for no other reason than that I haven't explored all of the island in that direction. I have time, I think— the wolves never appearing until after dark, the boat and the beach holding little appeal today, my arms already sore. From what, I wonder? The rowing? The pile of wood stacked to the side of the tiny house? The hole dug out back—its purpose still unknown?

North.

I remember there being something green on the horizon, from past reconnaissance, and as I head in that direction, it only takes an hour to find the apple orchard, a variety of fruit on display. There are some apples on the ground, but most are still waiting to be plucked—Golden Delicious, is what the first group looks like, the yellow apples glistening like tiny suns. Next to that are shiny dark red fruit, scandalous in their depiction of sin and desire—McIntosh, or Fuji, perhaps. Beyond those are a mottled-red variety, I think Honeycrisp—my favorite. They are crisp, and cold, and taste like heaven. I savor every bite.

I keep moving, the day filled with a gentle breeze, and the lilting song of birds I never actually see, always just out of sight, it seems—shadows at the periphery. Perhaps they are shy. Always something at the edges—my vision knitting together, pixels moving from scattered to tight, a shake of my head, and it all comes into focus. And just like that, a tiny bluebird flutters into my line of sight, looping in a circle, and then there are two, then six, then a hundred, and I slow my pace, back off a bit, the cloud of twittering taking on an air of violence. They move as one, washing over the air like a giant stroke from a paintbrush, and then they collapse in on themselves, back down to six, then two, then one. And then—*ping*, gone.

I have seen other animals on the island—the wolves up close and personal, circling the hut, teeth gnashing, the musky smell of their wet fur and hunger rising off their emaciated frames in waves. I have huddled in the darkness as lightning struck all across the island, running all the way down to the earth, scorching the long grasses, splitting trees where they stand, frying startled frogs to a crisp. And in the distance the sound of engines—so far up into the sky that I have to blink and squint, listen carefully as I try to track the tiny dots, a thin white trail etched across the blue. But today there is only the sunshine. I make a mental note to pay attention to the time, vowing to head back at the halfway point, in order to beat the darkness back to the little house.

And I do.

The days spill out one after another—caves to explore, where I find a cauldron of simmering macaroni and cheese, inexplicably bubbling over with goodness; a pile of golf balls on the top of the cliffs to the west, a single driver leaning up against an aging oak, the small white orbs teed up and driven into the ocean, at an increasing pace, until my arms are weak and glistening with sweat; the wood from the pile stacked high into a tower, a funeral pyre, in the middle of a circle made of stones, kindling snapped and funneled into the chimney, the flames licking high into the night, as I sit beside it, humming tunes with no name and no words.

I don't question any of it.

When I get a sunburn—the skin on my nose and lips delicate and dotted with pain—I ignore it. I find some aloe in a garden of herbs behind the house, and snap the greenery open, rubbing the softness over chapped lips and flaking skin. I'm not sure how much it helps. When I feel a presence at my ears, at night, while trying to fall asleep—something rustling by my head, sniffing, licking—I push it away, a mosquito most likely, my hand waving in the air, annoyed. When I undress by a waterfall on the back side of the cliffs, cleansing my dusty flesh with the cold, clear water, I see a series of scratches up and down my legs, across my forearms, and it startles me at first—until I remember the fields I'd walked through that day, the grass and bushes, the thorns and branches of the forest as well, the thin cuts stinging as I close my eyes. I ignore the alarms going off in some distant place and time, the tiny red flags I see planted along the dirt paths, the fireworks that fill the back of my eyelids when I go to sleep at night.

One day soon after that, I collapse in a field of tall grass, suddenly out of energy, as the sun sets over the horizon, the night slipping over the edge of the cliffs like a tsunami made of failure and buried secrets, motes dotting the edges. It feels so good to surrender to the gravity, the weight of it all suddenly too heavy to carry, the clover and dandelions a faint whisper of bounty. Above, the night sky is dotted with white pinpricks. I wait for the moon to fill with tainted light, for faces to appear in its surface. Fireflies flicker in the expanding darkness, the howl of the wolves in the distance bringing a smile to my face.

I'm not alone, I whisper into the earth. I'm not.

• • •

Back in my apartment, my gray-and-white cat paws at the goggles, licking my face, eventually taking a hesitant nibble, then a more desperate bite—starting with the tip of my nose, and then moving on to my chapped, silent lips.

13.

UNDONE

. . . AND WHEN WE TURN OFF into the woods I know it's a mistake, abandoning the road, the highway that has stretched out into the darkness for days now, the sun a distant memory, even though there has been nothing in the rearview mirror for miles, for hours, that choice is what makes all the difference, what cements our demise, Xina, and I, a couple for only as long as the night spilled across the land, for as long as the rest of our kind disappeared, and they filled in every inch of our existence in winged flocks that scattered and remade themselves, in the water where they schooled and wove between all other swimming creatures, in the earth where they burrowed deep into the dirt and soil, and then the corners of every room, every frame, shadows that spilled and expanded, never quite in our line of sight, but never quite gone either, Xina, with her red hair that fanned out behind her like flames, Xina, with her piercing green eyes that had shifted from jealousy to panic to fear to survival, Xina, as she tumbled out the car door, smoke unfurling out of the hood, something ticking from under the metal frame, the Nova getting us so far from everything, and yet not really buying us much time at all, not *really*, her door popping open first and mine second, a cloud of dust filling our lungs as the dirt road and gravel and weeds fill in around us, the end of the road, the fence there locked and chained, the forest looming up and out as the only place we might possibly find cover, the single path between two ancient oak trees that bend toward each other, as Xina and I seek each other out in our frantic loping toward the foliage, glancing back, nothing quite yet appearing—but soon, we know, soon—so we keep going, and as we grasp for each other, off into the trees, Xina trips and falls, and a sweat of panic washes over me as her swollen belly distends, her arms outstretched, hands that have nails bitten to the quick, no longer in my grasp, nothing I can do now but watch, and breathe, my heart hammering my rib cage, her scream something we should not release into the night, but her reaction is one of instinct, trying to brace her fall, and when I realize that she's going to lose the baby, when I glance back and see a scattering of leather wings across the night, flicking moonlight into the air, a fluttering rising up to drown out her cries, I know I have to keep going, and she knows it too, sobbing into the dirt, hands to her stomach, and below that, between her legs, her eyes wide, as I smell the blood, and it's just the one nod she gives me—my name muttered for perhaps the last time ever, *Malaki*—but it's enough for me to not even slow my pace and instead quicken it, leaping over her as I whisper how sorry I am, as I cry out to her, asking for forgiveness, as the smell of something foul fills the space between her and me and them—I keep moving, a stitch in my side, a tightness in my chest, because she's not the only one who's pregnant, not the only host here, and that's something else entirely that keeps bubbling up to the surface, one layer of tension the way that she might give birth in the woods, or a stream, or the back of the car, but another entirely different swelling of alarm the way that I will bring my child into the world, no obvious way for it to happen, not built for this, the agreement we made months ago something that was noble and obvious and not even up for debate until now, when I feel the kick, when I feel the bile rising, once more glancing back, this time to the ground cracking, and something slithering out in waves, and I'm into the trees, no longer going to look back, because I'm *it*, the last one, and it won't be long now, one way or the other, so I run, eyes on the path, slashes of pale moonlight splitting the forest in dazzling motes and beams of diminishing hope, moving forward, not familiar with this part of the state, this part of the country, but the smell of something musty in the air, as a cool breeze pushes through the bending trees, and I think *water*, maybe, it might be water, but I'm running so fast, breathing so hard, that it's hard to hear over my own desperate noises, my own gasping for air, heart rattling out a beat that has to slow, has to stop sometime soon, but not yet, not quite yet, and then I see it on the left, and then to the right, something pacing me in the trees, weaving in and out of the branches, the bushes, the cairns of rocks, and I curse the darkness, knowing I'm not nearly enough for this—up to it, capable, anything special at all—but if I can only hold on a bit longer, and my foot hits a root, and I stumble, as it's *my* turn for my eyes to go wide, for my hands to push out bracing for the fall, but I right myself and stagger up a hill, desperate to see the path, down another swell, and the pain in my gut expands, something tearing, and I cry out, my silence no longer mattering really, as they close in, shadows and snapping branches, the sound of something heavy ripping out by the roots, a flash of white just caught for a moment to my right, the snapping of teeth, so long and so sharp, the canopy of the forest rustling as something spills over the top of it all now, blocking out what little sick light was breaking through the leaves, and I can see now that the forest is coming to an end, it's a clearing up ahead, and that's not a good thing, out in the open, but I can go faster perhaps, if I don't simply split open before I get there, if my heart doesn't explode in a final fury, lungs withered in obsolescence, and then I hear it, what I thought I smelled before, *water*, something running fast and surely cold, the trees finally ending, as the field opens up, the tall grasses swaying back and forth as I fly into the open space, and across it, gnats and crickets leaping and spraying the air, and a handful of lightning bugs appears, causing me to clutch at my gut, to weep openly now as I continue to run—my knees burning, feet throbbing, arms covered in a slick sweat—no jar for me tonight, no tin foil and holes punched with a rusty screwdriver, and I laugh a harsh bark into the expanding gloom, unable to breathe or swallow, my insides twitching, and I only need to hold on a bit longer, to give my child a fighting chance here, as the grass cuts at my legs, risking one last look back, and that's a mistake, because they're here now, filling the space behind me, gaining, so close, and the only chance I have now is if what I heard, what I smell, is what I hope it is, not just *water*, but space and a bit more time, a few more seconds, and then I see it—the end of the field, the water below rushing by, bellowing in its cold ambivalence, and I hit the edge of the cliff as their stench drifts to me, foul and rotten, something sour and spoiling, and then I leap into history as my flesh rips, and my child finally emerges, pushing out, splitting me open, and I help it to come into this world, already crying, both of us, as my hands, my fingers feel for the edge of the tear, pulling wider, opening the gap, and it is beauti-ful in its horror, everything I could never be, nothing we have been before—unfurling one appendage after the other, several wings flapping open, unfolding again and again, talons lost in the black of night, a gleam in its myriad of eyes, placed in a close cluster atop its elongated head, neck extending as its jaw unhinges, row upon row of teeth chattering in anticipation, and then the last of it comes free, the tail pulling out longer and lon-ger, never seeming to end, the scales that cover it shimmering as the moon drifts out from behind a cluster of clouds, and I fall, knowing my work is done, but I'm wrong that my name was not uttered again, merely a different name this time, something I'd always longed to be, for it whispers my name, *Father*, as the rocks below rush up to me, the cold river undulating, the black mass descending, and when its wingspan fully unfurls, it blocks out the moon with an echoing finality.

14.

RING OF FIRE

"Have I told you about the monkeys?"

"Yes, several times."

"I have?"

"Yes."

"And?"

"And what?"

"You believe?"

"We're here, aren't we?"

"True."

"How long has it been?"

"Years?"

"Decades."

"Yes."

"Let's see how it's going."

"All of them? Or just him? This one?"

"Him, I think."

"It can happen in an instant, though, right?"

"So you've said."

•••

It's hard not to think about Rebecca all the time, while I sit here in the frozen tundra, running tests on rare compounds and minerals. She's the only human contact I have with the outside world, and the waiting is torture. I'm desperate for company, for her presence, and I long to see her—that radiant smile, those twinkling eyes, her melodious voice.

Some days it threatens to consume me.

Today, like every day, I've pulled a sample up from the vein that lies hundreds of feet directly below me. It's a complicated process, and I don't understand everything they're asking me to do here, but I have pride, so I do the work.

Not everything is clear, here.

They don't tell me much.

In order for me to be placed in this concrete bunker without windows, to keep me from losing my mind, they had to make some alterations—there were conditions to my contract, our agreement. The nanotechnology in my skull allows for partial memory erasure, as well as other things. So there may be a wife and kids waiting back home for me, wherever that is, or there may be nobody at all.

I don't know.

They say it's to keep me focused, so my mind doesn't wander.

Things have gone wrong before, it seems.

Top secret information, these details.

They say a lot of things.

Most days, I'm not even sure who *they* are. That's part of it too.

I signed up for this.

I think.

By my records, I have less than a year left, 288 days. Then the veil will be lifted.

We're a two-day drive from any form of civilization, the conditions so bleak, so cold, that there are times when planes can't even fly here—wings freezing, engines stalling, tires blown out when landing on the runway. On average, it's twenty degrees below zero, with a wind chill that dips down to negative forty, or sixty, even lower. It's dangerous out there—deadly. You can die of exposure in five minutes.

Or so I've been told.

I'm not sure exactly where I am.

• • •

The first time I met Rebecca, it did not go well.

I was having trouble adjusting.

While there is technology all around me, it fails constantly—computers and communication systems losing their connection, the signals and wavelengths unable to penetrate the elements, satellites futile, lines down everywhere; doors sticking, freezing, having to manually override them and physically turn levers, and gears, the exertion and stress draining; the solar panels covered with snow and ice, the windmill no longer turning, the bunker thrown into darkness, backup generators weak and unreliable.

When she pounded on the exterior door, I was in bad shape—no lights, freezing cold, alone. I . . . overreacted.

I didn't know who she was, so bundled up, male or female. I was just desperate for contact, of any kind.

There was no introduction: I just grabbed her, hugged her, babbling on and on. She pushed me away. There was a device, a taser of sorts.

I guess she was scared.

I'm sure this wasn't the first time something like this has happened.

When I woke up, she was gone, the samples taken.

But before I fully regained consciousness, before I could move, I felt something crawling over my arm—a spider, I think. And there was nothing I could do.

I hate spiders.

Sweat beaded up on my forehead, as its tiny legs lifted and then set down, lifted and then set down, inch by inch, up my arm, getting closer to my shoulder, and my face.

My mouth.

I tried to turn my head, slowly, my vision blurry, but I couldn't really move yet. The only thing I could do was blow on it.

So it bit me.

She said something, though, Rebecca, before leaving me there lying on the cold concrete. There was an echo in my head, a memory.

"No," she said, her voice soft, whispering in my ear. "This is not how we do this, Mark. We are professionals. Adults. Human beings. See you in thirty days."

I can remember just a hint of something sweet and musky—her perfume, I think. A touch of wintergreen—her breath.

"I believe in you," she said.

When she returned in a month, I stood in the center of the room, trembling. I waited for her to enter—the lights on this time, everything running smoothly—and held out my hand.

She shook it.

"Cold out there," I said, awkward and lost.

"It is."

She smiled, and I was able to breathe.

She became my world.

• • •

When I look in the mirror today, as I'm shaving, I notice my hair is starting to get gray. There are wrinkles around my eyes.

• • •

Because the minerals are so rare, so hard to find, the locations are secret. It's on a need-to-know basis—and I guess I don't need to know. Tiny amounts are harvested by a relatively simple drill, and extraction tube, but it must be processed and tested by hand. That's my job. Like a thread of saffron, the elements I touch are worth a lot of money. But I'm not the only one doing this kind of work.

I think.

I guess.

Saffron at $65 a gram is worth about $29,000 a pound. If the drill is working right, and nothing freezes, I pull a pound a day. At saffron prices that's almost $900,000 a month; $10.6 million a year.

By me.

Just me.

This dull, flat compound, somewhere between silver and platinum in color, is worth much more than that.

Much more.

When Rebecca shows up for her monthly visit, it is by some sort of vehicle, which I've never seen, her transportation parked beyond the walls of my tiny living quarters. To go beyond the grounds, to try to scale my encampment, would be death—in minutes.

There are days I consider it.

There are days that I hear howling in the distance, as I stand over the metal tube that is thrust deep into the frozen ground, pressing the button to pull up the sample, the timer on my wristwatch set to sixty seconds, the grinding of gears, the windmill overhead spinning and turning, slicing the air, the solar panels reflecting light, as I stomp my feet and smack my gloved hands together, goggles on, layers of clothing under a bright orange jumpsuit.

Or it could just be the wind.

It could be me.

• • •

Indium, tellurium, adamantium, cryolite, kashalt, palladium, etrium, hascum, rhodium, fepronor, soskite, veskin.

• • •

It's on a daily basis that I pull up about a pound of the raw material. It is a core sample that is found in tiny amounts, devices they never showed to me, or explained to me, going about their business deep below my location—scouting, drilling, digging, mining, and then packing it tight into a container that is shoved into a tube, and then raised up out of the frozen earth to a container about twenty feet behind my living quarters. When it's all working, the tube uses air to whoosh this sample up to me. When it's *not* working, I turn a crank, and a series of chains, I'm told, turns and rotates, pulling the valuable resource up and out of the ground. I work up a sweat on those days, the timer on my watch counting down.

Back inside, I sit at a metal table, and process the element.

I divide the quantity into thirds.

The first third is left raw, a consistency somewhere between dirt, clay, and stone. I cut, chip, and sort the mineral into tiny silver ramekins, weighing out each sample to no more than 0.5 ounces. Solid chunks, dust, or flakes—it doesn't matter.

The second third I put into a metal bowl, where I add water, and mix it by hand. I push and pull, knead the material, until I get it to the consistency of putty. Then I roll it out into tiny, thin threads—about the thickness of bucatini, no, a little less, more like spaghetti. I set it aside to let it dry, or sometimes place it in the microwave that sits on the counter to my right, a wall of shelves and cabinets filled with supplies. I have to be able to break the pieces, with just one finger, pushing down on the stalks, until they snap in half. Like ripe asparagus, feeling for the point of tension, the place the stalk severs in two. Then I fill the ramekins, again, each one under 0.5 ounces, as much as I can get into the tiny container.

I feel like a child, with my Play-Doh. If I sneeze, and mineral dust flies off the table in a puff, I say, "There goes five grand." Sometimes I laugh out loud.

The last third I also mix in a bowl, adding water until it is soft enough, liquid enough, to push through a sieve, filling the remaining ramekins, weighing them in at under 0.5 ounces, the gray pudding giving off a bitter, metallic scent.

This is my life.

Day after day.

It's no wonder I'm suicidal.

No wonder Rebecca is always on my mind.

While I'm breaking apart the mineral, rolling out the substance, pushing it through the screen, I think of her piercing green eyes, her long black hair, and her pale skin, like marble, shot through with nearly invisible turquoise veins.

I'm sure I'm one of many stops. I assume I'm not the only lab rat out here. But I've never seen anyone else. I'm certainly nothing to her, a package to be picked up, a package to be delivered.

When I'm especially sad and lonely, I manufacture a glimmer in her eye. Something that tells me to try again, that she likes me.

Over time this fiction becomes truth.

In my head.

The only place it matters.

• • •

"It's encouraging, right?"

"We've been here before. This part is easy."

"Yes, I know, but . . ."

"Too early to tell."

"But . . . the spider . . ."

"Yes?"

"He didn't kill it this time."

"That's true."

"That could mean something."

"Or it could mean nothing at all."

• • •

Not for the first time, I awake covered in blood.

I take the sheets from my bed and walk to the laundry room, strip naked, and then head for the shower. I check my body for scrapes, cuts, bruises, bullet holes, knife wounds, blisters, scabs—nothing. As I get dressed, I check every orifice—mouth, nose, ears, penis, anus—gently probing, tissue blown into, squeezing—nothing.

I wander toward the kitchen, to put the coffee on, and when I toss the old grounds into the garbage, I see glistening flesh, bones, and sinew—something furry, something gleaming in the black plastic. I vomit on top of the remains and stand up straight.

I don't want to know.

Do I?

I close the bag, take it to the incinerator chute, and drop it in.

The lid closes with a metal *tang,* and I walk back to the kitchen.

Sometimes I prefer to be left in the dark.

This memory will fade in time.

Mostly.

• • •

The footprint of the compound is small. Really, I shouldn't even call it a compound, but it's a word that pops into my head. Facility, lab, living quarters, station—jail. All the same, really.

There is the entry, with the thick metal door and its constantly jamming mechanisms, a series of levers and one giant metal wheel, for when it all fails. Everything here has a backup system that is solely reliant on my presence and physical strength. There is essentially one large room as you enter—the lab and kitchen off to the right, a sort of living room with a couch and television set in the middle, a table to the far left with four chairs (FOUR, I tell you, which will never all be used at the same time, goddammit), and toward the back—my living quarters, with a solitary bed, a bathroom and shower off to one side, cut back into the wall. There is storage up and down the walls—the equipment and supplies I need for my work, cabinets in the kitchen stocked with a year's supply of MREs, and then various chutes for disposal.

It's nothing to write home about.

Today, though, I found something.

In the back of a closet that runs alongside my bed, there were marks. Behind my requisite orange jumpsuits, all hanging up like the shed skin of long-dead molting astronauts, was a series of marks in the wall. Lines. One, two, three, four, the fifth across at a diagonal. Small, easy to miss, keeping track of something.

As I pushed the suits to the side, there were more. Not just the five, but a row of fives. And then several columns below. Rows and columns—a grid. I started to count and then got a bit dizzy, had to sit down. Dozens. Hundreds. Down the wall, as far as I could see.

I bent over, and took my pocket knife out of a zippered suit pocket.

I found the very end of the markings, dust filling into the cracks, cobwebs in the corner, but my little friend nowhere to be seen.

"Hello, there! I'm going to call you Charlotte."

I didn't make these marks.

I don't *remember* making these marks.

I count again.

Somewhere around three thousand and change, I stop.

I add a mark to the end.

I count again.

3,246.

Plus one.

Let's see where this goes.

• • •

Tristan da Cunha, Saint Helena; Motuo, Tibet; Ittoqqortoormiit, Greenland; McMurdo Station (Ross Island), Antarctica; Rapa Nui (Easter Island), Chile; Kerguelen Islands (Southern Indian Ocean); Pitcairn Island, South Pacific; Hawaii; Oymyakon, Siberia; Socotra Island (Yemen).

• • •

Everything was going fine, just fine. Rebecca decided to stay now, and we shared an MRE and chatted. I didn't care what she had to say; it didn't really matter. I just wanted to be close to her, to bask in her radiance. It was everything to me, that human contact, and I'd store up all those precious few minutes for later, when I was alone. Her smile, her laugh, the way she'd brush crumbs off her shirt. I was starving for the female form, her hand on my shoulder as she left sending electricity through my body, the crossing and uncrossing of her legs a flush of heat across my skin, and finally, after months of visits, a hug, as she departed.

I was a teenager, reduced to some base animal, so hungry for affection that I'd chew my own arm off.

I know I held her too long; I could feel the smile slip off her face as I nuzzled closer, inhaling her scent. I wanted to kiss her. Her hand on mine at the table, laughing at my joke: did I misinterpret her actions?

What right did I have to do this?

It felt like I had waited long enough. Months now.

I kissed her.

She did not kiss me back.

I opened my mouth to apologize, but I couldn't speak.

What had I done?

What had I undone?

"Mark," she exhaled, her face flushing, and then going pale, something sickly and green running under the surface of her skin. "Mark, no."

I didn't let go, though she was pushing away.

"I thought . . ."

"Let me go, Mark."

"It's been months now, hasn't it? Don't you enjoy my company? Tell me you don't feel the same way and . . ."

"I don't feel the same way, Mark," she said, still pushing at me, trying to break my hold. "All of our progress," she whispered, teeth bared. Tears formed in her eyes. And then she slapped me, her hand across my face like a gunshot, and I let go.

And in an instant, she was gone.

I don't know how the rabbit got in. Did she leave the door open? I had trouble remembering the days that followed, everything that led up to the next month. I ran my fingers over the bite mark on my hand, the scar that was forming, and cursed the furry monster.

I hoped she would come back. Give me a chance to explain.

A chance to apologize.

She had to come back, right? This was her job.

I could change.

I could wait.

• • •

"Reset?"

"Again."

"Not even as far as last time."

"No. But the spider . . ."

"Didn't make a difference."

"You sure?"

"Did you see the rabbit?"

"I did."

"Again?"

"Yes. Again."

• • •

The first time I met Rebecca, I stood in the center of the room, trembling. I was so excited for company. I didn't care who it was. I waited for her to enter—the lights on, everything running smoothly—and held out my hand.

She shook it.

"Cold out there," I said, awkward and lost.

"It is."

She smiled, and I was able to breathe.

She became my world.

I was excited to show her the rabbit; Bugs, I called him. I didn't tell her about the spider in the closet, or the fact that I spoke to Charlotte when I was lonely, late at night. Rebecca didn't need to know that yet.

There was so little around me here, so little life, but it seemed to find me. It sought me out, and we found a way to make it work. We respected each other's space, and that seemed to work just fine.

• • •

Goldfish, hermit crab, hamster, tarantula, turtle, mouse, lizard, snake, fish, kitten, puppy, parrot, guinea pig, ferret, rabbit.

• • •

By my records, I have less than a year left, 288 days.

Things are going well with Rebecca. I asked her to stay longer, last time, and she complied. This has been slowly improving, every time she visits. She doesn't mind that my hair is almost entirely gray.

Mostly we talk. I like to hear what she has to say, though she won't tell me much about the outside world.

Contract.

Rules.

And that's fine.

She checks on the tube and box outside when she first arrives, and I often stand at the door and watch her. There is just that one tiny slot of glass, but I can see out, as long as it isn't covered in snow and ice. She works so hard. I have a lot of respect for her, the way she is fearless in her expedition, the discovery and exploration of this barren, frozen land. She asks about the samples, and we discuss things like viscosity, breaking point, and yield. She seems to be encouraged by the minerals I'm harvesting, the product, but beyond that she grows more kind and intimate.

It's been a gradual shift, months now, as we get closer to the end of my contract. She asked me if I'd stay on longer. Threw out a hypothetical. I want to believe it's because she enjoys my company, in addition to the resources we're finding here.

But I don't want to jump to conclusions.

She stayed longer today, more than the requisite five minutes, longer than the fifteen it took to fix the excavation tube, longer than it took to help stock my supplies, nearly thirty minutes.

If I didn't know any better, I'd say she was stalling.

We sat on the couch today and played cards. She took off her jumpsuit and stayed for almost an hour. She said she was hot, usually in and out in a few minutes, no need to take off her gear, back out into the elements.

She sat so close to me, Bugs hopping around at our feet. She brought a few carrots this time, for the rabbit, and we fed the furry beast between hands of Go Fish and War. The little bugger is so cute when he wiggles his nose, chewing away, his eyes sparkling with secrets.

When Rebecca leaned in and kissed me, I was surprised. It was a heady moment, having been alone for so long, the body of a woman so close to me, I thought I might burst into flame. My heart was pounding in my chest, her hands on my face as she gently placed her lips on mine, her soft breath wintergreen, her lips parting as her tongue slid into my mouth, the moisture and delicacy of her embrace sending electricity across my skin.

When she pulls back for a moment, she smiles.

"I've been dying to do that," she whispers.

"I've been dead until this moment," I reply. "This . . . resurrection."

She laughs.

Her hands are on my shoulders, mine on her arm, her leg.

"I have to go," she says.

"I know."

"I'm sorry, it's a long drive. . . ."

"It's okay," I say. I understand.

She smiles and lowers her gaze.

"Could you just kiss me one more time?" I ask. "Something to remember you by, over these next thirty days."

I inhale, and she fills me with her essence—pomegranate, jasmine, amber, and patchouli.

"Yes."

She leans in, and that one kiss turns into several, but soon enough she stops, and stands, running her hands down her front, straightening out her shirt, her pants, smiling as she walks away.

"If I don't leave now, well, I may not be able to leave at all," she laughs.

I am blind with lust.

"At all!" she says. "At all!"

Her shoulders twitch, and she blinks her eyes, but I'm not looking at her; I'm breathing in deeply, closing my eyes, willing her to stay.

Or to hurry back.

"I'm not going anywhere," I joke.

"And we have more work to do," she says.

"Yes. The work," I say.

"I know where you live," she jokes.

"Yes, you do."

I watch her pull on her orange jumpsuit, putting on more clothes, the opposite of what I want, my desire and longing bubbling to the surface. I try to breathe again, but it's not easy.

"You going to see me out?" she asks.

"Not sure I can stand up right now."

She blushes a little and runs her hand through her hair.

"I'll get a glass of water, then. That enough time for you to cool off?"

"Hopefully."

And she gets the glass of water, holding it to her lips, but not actually drinking. The level stays the same.

I don't notice.

I'm thinking about other things, trying to envision the future, one that involves slick flesh, and darting tongues, and I can still taste her in my mouth—salty and sweet.

I stand.

"Let's get you on the road, then."

She takes my hand, and I walk her to the door.

• • •

"Encouraging."

"Very."

• • •

There is a flash of light, and a series of images flows across my line of sight. It scrolls forward, this little movie, and I see so many things, all in black and white. I see a much younger version of myself, and he seems to be having a lot of trouble with nature. I am still here in this lab, and between the interactions with a series of animals, there is Rebecca walking in the door, Rebecca walking out, Rebecca sitting down at a table, playing cards and eating meals with my thinner, more vibrant self. There is a spider at my neck, and I slap at it, killing it dead, looking at my hand, grimacing as a pulsing dot rises to the surface. There is a scene where a rabbit, much like Bugs, bites my hand and doesn't relax its grip on me, its teeth deep, blood spurting onto the floor, as I turn and run in circles, eventually slamming it against the concrete wall, the creature finally letting go, falling to the ground like a sack of bruised potatoes. And there is more Rebecca—she is pushing me away, she is slapping my face, she is stunning me with a taser, she is sliding a knife in and watching me slump to the floor. And then we are back to the front door, where a wolf slinks in on gray padded feet, teeth bared, as I spin and look for escape, none to be found, latched on to my arm as I beat it with my fist, the animal lunging for my neck, and then suddenly darting out the door.

There is something with a polar bear. I have a hard time watching. I can't take the screaming. The claws across my chest, the mouth on my arm and hand as I try to push it away, the beast filling the space of the tiny lab, shaking its head back and forth, biting down on my hand, ripping it off, my body jolting, eyes rolling back in my head, my hand severed at the wrist, the massive creature sitting on me, drool rolling out of its gaping jaws, and then it sits up, braying at the room, finally rising up on all four legs, turning its head, and sauntering out the door.

I wake up in my bed covered in sweat.

Not blood.

I flick on the light and run my hands over my body, searching for a remnant from the screening I've just witnessed—fingers gently touching my throat, my arms, my chest, my legs.

Nothing.

I check my watch, and it reads 3:10 a.m.

As my fingers run under my left wrist, massaging a phantom pain, the wrist the bear severed, I feel a ridge of a scar running all the way around. It's hidden under the watch. It's very thin. I wonder if I'm imagining it, but when I take off the watch, I can see how it rings my arm, my flesh.

From here, or something else entirely?

I don't know.

I flex my hand, and it feels fine.

I stand up and head to the kitchen, the lights low, the bunker quiet.

I take a knife out of a drawer and push the tip into the heel of my hand.

Nothing.

I push deeper, and it punctures my flesh.

Nothing.

I pull it out, and blood spills onto the counter.

I breathe a sigh of relief, and I'm not sure why.

• • •

Veggie burger, beef enchilada, chicken fajita, chili mac, maple sausage, chili with beans, cheese tortellini, beef ravioli, meatballs in marinara, chicken a la king.

• • •

There are cameras hidden everywhere, but I don't notice them until much, much later. Discovering them explains a lot of things, but not everything. Not even close.

• • •

At the back of the compound, beyond the tube and mechanical equipment, there is a wall. There are walls on all three sides that go up a good fifteen feet, maybe more. I can't see over or beyond them, the only thing above me the blue sky, an occasional cloud, and the rare plane flying high overhead, like a spider crawling slowly across the ceiling. At the far end of the grounds, this tiny plot of land, there is a door. It's how Rebecca enters my humble abode. I've never opened it, not once.

Today I do.

It is so cold . . .

or so I've been told

. . . that I can only be outside for a short period of time. The time I set on my watch is for one minute, but much like the tall metal door embedded in the concrete wall, I've never thought to challenge it.

Why?

Bundled up, I head out the back of my prison to the machine, where I push the button, the tube rattling, noises rumbling up from below the frozen surface. I walk past the device, to the tall, icy door that stands between myself and . . .

What?

Oblivion?

I assume cold, snow, ice, and wind. What else could there be?

My stomach growls, and I walk on.

The timer is ticking down, so I pick up the pace, a glance over my shoulder as the minerals are brought to the surface, closing the distance to the wall, and the door, in no time. My glove on the handle, I turn it and pull the heavy metal door open.

What lies beyond?

There is wind, and snow, ice particles stinging my face, blinding me, and as I stand there, taking a step into the unknown, a wave of nausea washes over me, a sour sweat breaking out on my forehead, goggles fogging up, bile rising. I swallow and take a step forward, the clock in my head cleaving brutal seconds out of my desire, another step, and I drop to one knee, pulling down my ski mask, my scarf, vomiting into the snow.

I cannot see. The wind, the ice, it might as well be another wall, ringing this one, and then one beyond that, and then one beyond *that*, panic rising to the surface, a diseased rat trapped in the center of a never-ending maze.

I wipe my goggles clumsily with my oversized gloves, and through a momentary pause in the storm, the ice, and snow, I see something else, something moving, a dark shadow in the white. It's moving toward me, first on two legs, then down on four, then it's levitating, off the surface, drifting to me, rolling, undulating. Light bisects the gauze—floating, bobbing. I smell oil and gasoline, and there is the sound of an engine, the slamming of a door, somewhere in the distance, and then a voice, much closer.

"Let's get you inside."

I cannot see, my head stuffed with cotton, my gut writhing with snakes.

"It's not safe out here," she whispers.

And then we're standing.

She wasn't due for three more days.

Lumbering back inside the door to the compound, it slams shut, and she pushes me forward, holding my arm, keeping me up, and she is strong.

Very strong.

As we pass the tube, she lifts the lid and takes out the sample, all without breaking stride. Without breaking a sweat, I assume.

Somewhere between the equipment, the door, and the interior of my bunker, I pass out. When I wake up on the couch, I am lying down, a cold compress on my head, and she is handing me water—cold, crisp water that goes down like tiny knives, filling my gut with a detached certainty.

Rebecca is smiling at me, but her eyes are dancing, a troubling chaos of buzzing motes and escalating fear.

"You're okay," she says. "I'm glad I came by early, the storms in the area are getting worse. I may be trapped here for a while. Was trying to beat them south. Guess I lost *that* race."

I nod.

She leans over and hugs me, whispering in my ear.

"You don't want to wake up, do you?"

• • •

Sonder, conform, stay, transform, control, cocoon, equality, truth, trust, oblivion, restraint, love, door, kuebiko.

• • •

Rebecca does stay, and it's the best thing that has ever happened to me. As far as I can remember. Which is only a few months. Actually 167 days, I think. Back to the day I arrived here, I assume by plane, and some sort of rugged-terrain vehicle, six wheels, windows on all sides, strapped in—there are images, and I try to fill in the blanks, but I can't be sure.

There are moments when my skin hums, and I feel on fire, fighting so hard for control. She is a gift, Rebecca, I know that, and I cherish every moment of our time together—playing cards, holding hands, eating the horrible MREs, watching movies—but there is something off. She is beautiful, but at times I feel as if we are teenagers. There is an innocence that is both welcome and disconcerting. There are times she looks at me, and her eyes are those of a child. Her body is so close, the heat she gives off, it ripples through my flesh, so hard to contain.

The storm continues outside.

It rages inside, as well.

When she stands and walks to the back of the room, off to take a shower, I swallow my desire and clench my fists.

I look over my shoulder and follow her gait, the movement of her body, as she slowly peels off one item of clothing after another.

She smiles over her shoulder—teasing me, testing me.

"Not yet," she whispered in my ear when we were pressed together, hands exploring bare arms, tongue and lips and the nape of her neck, her scent intoxicating.

She is making me wait.

And I'm not sure why.

She knows my desire, her hand on my pants, running up my thigh, a gleam in her eye as she squeezes my erection through my pants, her body pressed up against mine, this torture both blissful and cruel. When I run my hand up her arm and hold her breast in my palm, a thin layer of fabric between her flesh and mine, her eyes close, my thumb running over her erect nipple, her eyelids flickering, a gentle moan easing out of her parted lips.

And then she bolts up and heads to the shower, my head spinning, as she peels off her shirt, walking away from me, unclicking her bra and dropping it to the ground. Her skin is like alabaster, the heat in my hand fading, a cold wave of despair rushing in.

"I'm not ready," she says, her lips on my neck.

And I honor it.

For now.

But I'm only human.

The shower runs, steam billowing out of the open door, and I can see her shadow beyond the glass. I unzip my pants and pull out my cock, the tip glistening, and spit in my hand. Gliding up and down, my reddening flesh engorged, I finish with a startling quickness, spilling my seed on the concrete.

I am both horrified and released, but not satisfied.

I clean up my mess, get a drink of water, and pray to whatever gods exist to give me strength, to give me wisdom, to give me patience.

I don't want to screw this up.

• • •

Lying in bed, Rebecca whispers in my ear.

"I can help you. But you need to know. We've tried everything else, and nothing works. I think this is the only way."

I don't know what she means.

She sighs and starts to cry. Or maybe she's laughing. I can't tell.

"Your memories," she says, laying her head on my chest.

A flash of black-and-white still images runs across my eyelids, a repetition of tubes and minerals, and a zoo of animals, one after the other, biting me, tearing me to pieces—spiders, snakes, rabbits, wolves, and bears. It loops and nothing changes. There are the moments with Rebecca, a series of paths from the kitchen to the couch to the shower to the bedroom to the front door, over and over, back and forth, the concrete worn in the same lanes that we walk again and again, the predictable behavior, the ways we live this simple life. Beyond that is something else, but she's right, I can't see it—fog, smoke, haze, gauze, frosted glass, snow, ice, a digital wall of ones and zeroes blocking anything beyond this frozen bunker. Something else lurks in the shadows—bodies, flesh, cold, metal, the feeling of running, a wave of panic, a growing undulation of desire and then loss, sirens and lights, a city in the distance, voices, and then pain, blood, and a flash of white light, blinding me, and then scalpels, knives, bandages, and more whispering, more instructions. None of it can be held for more than a second, less than that, rushing past, none of it making sense, all of it out of focus.

"If you ask *me*, and they don't, it's no way for this to happen. To truly work," she says, and again I'm lost.

She raises her head and looks at me.

"I'm sorry; this makes no sense to you," she whispers, her eyes searching my face for emotion, her voice lowering, her lips now at my ear again, quieter, barely speaking.

"I have to show you. It's the only way for you to change."

I stare up at the concrete ceiling, the room dark, her body so close to me that she feels like an extension of my own flesh.

"Don't freak out," she says.

"What?"

"Just trust me."

"What are you talking about?"

She sighs. "Do you trust me?"

And I think about that. No, I don't.

Yes, I do.

I mean, as much as I trust anyone. And yet, there *is* nobody, so it's a small sample size.

Yes?

"Of course," I say, too slow.

"You don't. And that's okay. I mean, you do on some level, but not entirely. And that's fair. I trigger suspicion in so many ways."

I take another breath, and she runs her hand up and down my bare chest.

"Whatever happens next, can you just trust me?"

"Yes. Sure," I say. "Why not?"

And I laugh.

There are so many options, my schedule wide open, so many choices.

Sarcasm—it's one choice of many, and in this moment, I choose to trust her.

"Okay," she says.

She climbs on top of me, wearing nothing but a tank top and panties, straddling me, and I smile.

It's not at all what I expect.

She leans over to kiss me and whispers, "Don't scream," her mouth lowering to mine, her lips pressed up against mine, her strong hands on the sides of my head, gentle at first, and then gripping harder, her tongue in my mouth, her lips parting wider, and wider, and then I feel it.

Something crawls out of her throat, across her tongue, and into my mouth. My eyes go wide, and I try to close my mouth, but her hands are now at my face, prying my lips apart, the tiny creature with its many little legs walking around the inside of my mouth, tip-toeing across my tongue as I gag and struggle. The tiny, cold, mechanical feet probe and dance, piercing me gently, seeking purchase, and then it moves down my throat, her hands keeping my mouth open wide, her own eyes gleaming in the darkness, two moons afire, and I am choking, I can't breathe, the creature crawling into my throat and then up into my sinus cavity. I'm going to vomit, to sneeze, my eyes watering as it seeks its final destination.

When it gives birth, I pass out.

• • •

Awake or dreaming, real or imagined, I vomit into the toilet, mostly my dinner, but also mucus, and ribbons of blood. I pick tiny pieces of metal out of my teeth, spitting what looks like glitter into the basin. In my head, I hear her voice.

Dipole antenna, locomotion flagella, pneumatic connector, macromanipulator.

She may as well be speaking Russian.

Undoing.

Erasing.

Unlocking.

Remembering.

There are tissues in the garbage can that frighten me. Blood, discharge, flesh, and bits of metal. I stare at the yellow-and-green phlegm, the abstract Rorschach giving me no answers, splashes of red, bits of silver and black shimmering in the waste, a tiny light blinking.

When I look up, Rebecca is standing in the doorway. She turns her head to the left and then the right, looking for something.

She steps inside the doorframe and holds her finger to her lips.

"Shhhhhhhhhhhhhh," she says.

I look at the mess again, and this time I do see something— failing or passing the psych evaluation, I'm not sure. Cracked skulls, an alley littered with garbage, and a highway leading to a horizon rippling with fire.

• • •

Amur leopard, brown bear, flying squirrel, musk deer, weasel, chipmunk, tiger, reindeer, polar bear, fox, wolf, penguin, ermine, lemming, tern.

• • •

"Did you hear back?"

"Yes."

"And?"

"She checked. Wiring. Due for maintenance. Nothing major."

"We're not concerned, then, are we?"

"No, not yet."

"But we'll keep an eye on her. On them both."

"Yes."

"And the others?"

"Failures across the board."

"So, the tipping point?"

"Not even close, I'm afraid."

"Exponentially difficult."

"Definitely."

• • •

After Rebecca leaves, the storm supposedly over, I clean up the place a bit, walking in circles, thinking about everything that has happened lately. When I go to dump the bag of garbage down the chute, the button doesn't work. Next to the device is a tiny screen, and on it I see these words:

ERRROR 1404—JAM IN CHUTE

There is a series of tiny buttons next to the small screen, buttons I've never pushed before, so I scroll through, looking for choices, trying to troubleshoot the machine. I reset it, a series of rumbling noises emanating from the wall, clicking sounds, and then the screen goes dark. Rebooting, the message reappears.

I open the metal lid, and the bag I dropped in there the other day still sits there, blocking the chute. Or stacked up on a series of bags.

Turtles all the way down, I think.

I step back from the wall and *really* look at it for the first time. You'd think in my time here that I'd have explored every nook and cranny of this pathetic little world I live in, but I haven't. The metal chute is embedded in the wall, and I run my hands around the edges, looking for something—I'm not sure what: a panel, a door, anything that might help me fix this.

To the left of the metal, which runs from the floor to the ceiling, there is more metal, nothing special, just more steel, to go with more concrete that runs the length of the floor, and the walls, more inanimate, boring, common compounds. It's so dull, I could fall asleep just looking at this nondescript existence.

Running my hands over the wall, fingers in grooves, I notice a small square of metal about halfway up the wall, about the size of a deck of cards. I bend over to read the little letters:

PUSH

"Huh," I say out loud.

I push.

The panel flips open, and inside there is a handle, folded back into the small compartment. I reach in, grab it, and pull.

The wall in front of me creaks, and sticks, nothing moving, so I pull harder, and the entire panel, much larger than I originally thought, moves. It's tall, taller than me, what I think must be some sort of door. I pull again, and dust spills out, the metal panel opening wider, to reveal an opening, some sort of tunnel, I think, and a ladder leading down into the darkness.

Utility tunnel? Maintenance? News to me.

Maybe this is something that Rebecca knows about, something she checks, beyond my pay grade, not cleared for such information.

I head back over to the kitchen and rummage through the junk drawer. Yes, even here at the end of the world, there is a junk drawer. Pens, scissors, paperclips, and a flashlight. Several, actually. I click one on, and it works, the beam strong but flickering a bit, so I smack it with my hand, and the light solidifies.

Back to the opening I head.

The light isn't strong enough to penetrate the darkness, at least not all the way down, but as I feel around on both sides I locate a button and press it, halogen lights slowly coming on. I can see the ladder goes down quite deep, the floor below out of sight.

Why not.

I put the flashlight in a pocket of my orange jumpsuit and step into the space, turning around, and slowly lower myself down the ladder, committed to finding the bottom.

Down, and down, and down I go, but soon enough I find the bottom, the walls concrete, as dull and lifeless as the rest of my home. At the bottom, there is a large room that opens up to my right, and in the center of the space is an incinerator. It lies dormant, no light or heat, something wrong.

The lights down here are working, though, dull squares of flat illumination installed in the walls. I fish out the flashlight and search the black metal incinerator for buttons, instructions, levers, and doors. In the center of the large wall of metal is indeed a door, and a metal handle, with arrows pointing in one direction, so I turn the handle, and rotate it, the door coming open, and I pull it back to reveal the gaping maw of the machine.

Inside, there are bags, so many bags. It seems the incinerator hasn't been working for quite some time. The space is much bigger than I thought, the flashlight in my hand hardly penetrating the darkness, the back wall of the furnace out of sight.

I try to count.

So many bags.

I can only count a row, a wall of them, ten bags high by fifteen bags wide, or so I estimate. Then I try to multiply that by the depth, unable to see the back wall. Ten deep? Twenty? A hundred?

How long have I been here?

How long has *anyone* been here?

I close the door and find a series of buttons, as well as a tiny screen. I follow the instructions and then press a large green button that says IGNITE.

There is a *whooshing* sound, and a series of lights runs up and down the front, something happening, the heat from the incinerator pushing me away like a giant hand.

When I try to extrapolate the waste I've sent down, multiplying meals by other garbage by days—it doesn't compute.

Months.

Years.

Decades.

More.

I feel sick.

I scratch my head, try to breathe, and a few strands of gray hair, *white* hair, come away in my fingers.

I cough.

The heat is growing, so I back away and head up the ladder, my face in a permanent scowl.

Back at the chute, I close the door, click it shut, and open the lid, pushing the bag forward, listening to it slide down the metal opening, the heat rushing up, a smell of food waste, plastic, and something sour drifting up to me.

In my head there is a subtle buzzing; in my ears, a dull ringing—my gut filled with worms of unease.

I take a breath and close my eyes.

How long until Rebecca comes back?

• • •

She said to trust the spiders. To give it time. They would reveal things to me, she said, and I should pay attention.

It's starting.

I'm seeing things.

Remembering.

• • •

I was chosen. I realize that now.

At night, in the darkness, I can feel their tiny feet wandering through my skull, heading toward the chip, the implant, doing their little jobs.

What comes back to me washes over me in a wave.

There is a room, much like this one, only there is darkness that knows no end. It is cold, the isolation both a gift and a curse, a welcome separation from the world around me, and yet an undoing of my every human quality.

When the sensation of being watched starts, it is unmistakable. Alone for so long, the bundle of eyes that turn and focus, has a weight that settles over me like a blanket. And at first, I welcome the gaze.

It does not ask any questions, this presence, but I find it comforting, to not be alone for a moment.

But that will quickly change.

When it turns away, the cold seeps back in, and I sob in the endless pitch, floating in an ether of nothingness.

There is no desire, there is no hunger, only waiting, and uncertainty, a throbbing sadness that will not end.

I feel that I must have done something.

I do not deserve this for nothing.

And yet my mind is empty. It is a blank canvas, ready to be painted. It is dull clay, waiting to be molded. It is a disease in a petri dish, longing for a cure.

I simmer and rage against the darkness, to no avail.

When I finally do speak, I ask it to return. My throat is dry, my tongue cracked, unable to really say much of anything beyond a squeak and a cough and a wheeze.

Time stretches out in front of me like an endless, expanding black rubber band, both elastic and fixed, tactile and abstract. As much as I want to think, to feel, to question, and to understand—my mind remains blank.

I have no name, no past.

No future?

No memories.

Eventually it returns.

They return.

And in the moment, I feel as light as a feather, levitating off the cold, concrete bench, or bed, or cell—whatever this is, wherever I am. I am nude, and over my skin is a rippling of sensations, what starts out as tiny, rubber flagella, weaving and undulating, rustling under my body, raising me up, as if on a series of tentacles, my body limp and relaxed, floating in the air.

The strands pulsate and move, wrapping around my appendages, tighter and tighter. At first it's comforting, but quickly it changes to a sense of inquiry and constriction, as they circle my flesh and start to pull in different directions.

Something sharp pierces my skin, and I shriek out into the blackness. And then it happens again, and again, a series of needles, or teeth, rising to the surface of the tightening lengths of cold rubbery flesh, some quickly stabbing and retreating, others slower, pushing in slowly—sampling, probing, and extricating.

The pain, it is exquisite.

I am leaking something—the piercing, the stabbing, the tiny needles—tiny *teeth*—pulling out water, blood, and other fluids.

And something is being injected—a pulsing that rushes through my body, as if a great amount of liquid is being poured into me, the logistics and physics of it impossible, and yet it continues to fill me up, the sensation of swelling, of expanding, running over my arms and legs, my torso, my face.

When they start to pull again, my limbs stretching, my bones creaking, I open my mouth to protest, to scream perhaps, and a singular fleshy appendage pushes down my throat, blocking any sound. My eyes widen, and I cannot breathe. Tears stream down my face. My skin starts to chill, a sheen of ice building over my flesh, cascading toward the edge of a cliff, and there are three ways I can die now, all of them rushing to the surface—suffocation, quartering, and hypothermia.

I am raised and lowered, thrashing around in the darkness, the pain spiking and then retreating, as if caught by a giant squid, my skin turned to ice; up and down I go, cracks running across the surface of my body, higher and lower, my mouth, my throat, my stomach filled with a weight that is sour, and sticky, and then it happens.

I am shattered on the concrete—a long pulling sensation coming up and out of my body, the flesh that no longer exists—a flashing of lights, my sight both absent and then suddenly rushing to the surface, the smell of smoke, something burning, and then I hit the floor, again, solid.

I gasp for breath, crying in the darkness, begging for it to stop.

I am still held in its gaze as a bright light fills the room, blinding, so much worse than the darkness, for I can see it all now—my flesh, and sinew, and pulsing organs; the creature at the wall with the panoply of stacked, glistening eyeballs, its flesh covered in molting scales, tentacles raised as dull, black feathers spill into the air, a discharge of dark viscous liquid expelled from under its sulking presence, and then the void rushes back in, a welcome blindness, dancing yellow motes glowing and flickering, swarming around its hulking presence in a chaotic orbit, a sickly sweet smell of strawberries, and rotting meat, filling the room, a chorus of clicking claws, or beaks, a dull moan emanating from somewhere within the beast, the smell of wet fur, and then freshly cut grass.

And then it is gone.

Silence.

My every fear—manifest, incarnate—drowning, insignificance, weakness, dogs and wolves, spiders and insects, mirrors and ghosts.

There is a flicker, and the gaze returns.

There are voices in the darkness, whispers and promises, something cold and wet tonguing my ears, my hair standing up on end, goosebumps running across my flesh.

And I say "Yes."

To all of it.

I seek redemption, and forgiveness.

• • •

The next time I go to the door at the end of my property, my watch set to two minutes instead of one, there is no storm beyond it. I push through, and walk forward, fighting my panic, the nausea. And what lies beyond my walls, and that tall, metal door?

Another wall.

And another door.

To the left, a small path, the same to the right, bending around corners, my sight ending at the bend.

I lean over and retch, but nothing comes out, just a single strand of spit, with a smattering of tiny metal components dotting the snow.

A coin of blood falls from my nose, a payment to the ferryman, for a trip I cannot take. I rush forward to the second door, much like the first, the wall much higher, double in height, maybe more.

The door does not give.

The winds pick up, as if a giant fan has been clicked on, and the snow starts to fall, the ice stabbing at my goggles and clothes, the quiet quickly erased, replaced by a howling, the air rushing down the stretch of cordoned-off land, shadows running over the concrete dividers.

My watch alarm goes off, what little exposed skin I have frozen now, possibly dying.

I rush back in, close the door behind me, take my sample, and retreat to my home.

Overhead there is a sonic boom—a snap, and a crack in the atmosphere like huge sheets of ice breaking in half.

Something launches into the sky.

But I do not hear it.

Not today.

• • •

Castration, positive reinforcement, negative reinforcement, trepanation, hydrotherapy, electroconvulsive therapy, rui-katsu, ASMR, bloodletting, hydrotherapy, insulin shock, seizure therapy, orgone therapy, nanotechnology.

• • •

What could have been.

I often think about that.

The spiders have been doing their work. My nose has been bleeding more often, and I still cough up bits of gray flesh, often speckled with tiny gears, rods, and microprocessor fragments. Now and then there are other things that I can't explain—fragments of what must be teeth and fingernails—as if somehow I have absorbed another version of myself, a galactic battle inside some colossal womb.

They don't speak to me, as they nibble at my inner workings, but the chittering I hear in my sleep, when things are quiet, it could contain information. There is no Morse code, but still I listen and continue to sift through whatever waste comes out of my body, as if reading tea leaves, or coffee grounds, searching for meaning.

When they clamp down, when they chew into my gray matter, I often lose myself. I wake up in strange places—at the door, as if looking outside, searching for something, or someone; by the sink, the water running, as if preparing a meal, or perhaps washing up; on the couch, as tears run down my face, the scent of Rebecca just a memory, her ghost lingering, and I wonder if she was just here.

I don't want to wake up.

Rebecca was right about that.

It goes back, so very far back.

There was a cage, and a furry creature inside it—a hamster, I believe. I used to love to watch him run in circles, so futile. It made me laugh. I liked to feed him, to watch his nose wrinkle up, the way his little beady eyes would glow like two tiny pieces of coal. When I put him on the record player, he was able to keep up, at least at the $33\frac{1}{3}$ speed, less so as I cranked it up, to 45 rpm, the 78 flinging the little guy off into space. I didn't see my dog sitting there, wagging its tail, eyes wide open, panting. The black lab was a sweetheart, but she didn't hesitate—gulped it down with hardly a bite. It shocked me, and yet I applauded. Later she got sick. Because I was responsible for cleaning up the poop in the yard, it would only be a few days before I found the bones, tiny legs, a few little chicklets that must have been teeth. Part of me felt like vomiting. But part of me didn't. Part of me was intrigued.

The fire, that was an accident. Or it's what I tell myself. How often I found myself staring into the flames, the campfire flickering tongues of orange and red into the sky, hypnotic in their heat and allure. I'd spent all day building that fire, stacking thick logs at the bottom, and then building the chimney higher and higher, offsetting one log after the other, until it was a smokestack as tall as I was, a pyramid of fire. I spent hours breaking off twigs and filling it up. When we lit it that night, my friends and family gathered around, everyone excited to see how big it would get; there was a palpable excitement in the air. I was proud of what I'd made. We thought the branches above us were way too high, spread far enough apart to avoid it all.

We were wrong.

So high it blazed, that fire, up into the dark sky, our eyes raised to the heavens, the sparks and embers drifting on the slight breeze. The trees would catch fire in minutes. Buckets were brought, ladders and hoses, and we managed to prevent the flames from jumping to the other trees, from burning down the campgrounds. We all shared the blame. And I grinned in the darkness like a fool.

The girl was a neighbor, and she was the one who asked *us* to play. My brother and I went with her to the woods, to the gathering of bushes.

We were curious. What children aren't?

My brother. I forgot I had a brother.

I'd never seen it before, what a girl had to offer. I was scared, but she wanted to see ours too. So we tied her up to a tree that was hidden in a grove of bushes, raised her shirt and pulled down her shorts. It wasn't that impressive. We had nipples too. We showed her ours, when she asked, both of us limp. She shrugged. When my brother left, I kissed her, gently. And she smiled. We were so young. When I got hard, she noticed, nodding her head. It was starting to make sense. I didn't touch her, besides the kiss. I untied her, and she left, skipping and singing a tune. It was all very normal. Right?

These moments. Did they matter?

I don't know.

I suppose it's how the story is framed, my reaction, and what happened next.

Were there other incidents, involving a squirrel or a cat? Was there a fire the following summer, at the same camp, one that burned down acres of land? Did the girl come back and ask for the bushes again, and did I oblige? Did we learn more about each other that day?

I don't know.

I can't tell truth from fiction.

I'm a good man.

I was a good boy.

Not everything is black and white.

So many shades of gray.

When I come to, I'm sick to my stomach, a tension weaving through my head, my fingers at my temples, unsure of my actions, begging for forgiveness just in case.

I ask the spiders to stop.

I consider Rebecca's words again.

In the kitchen I find a long piece of metal, a skewer. For all those barbeques we have outside. I laugh as I slowly insert it into my left nostril and take a deep breath. This is delicate work. Up into my sinus cavity I push it, slowly, *so slowly*, bit by bit until I finally meet resistance. I hesitate in this moment.

It feels like the right thing to do. The clarity I'm getting is not the truth I want, it seems.

I make a fist with my other hand, the one not holding the skewer, and prepare to bang it through, measuring the distance once, twice. . . .

Inside my skull I feel metal on metal, one of the babies chittering at the spike of the skewer, but its plea falls on deaf ears. One *ping*, then another, several of them clamping onto the metal spike that is pushing against the wall of my sinus cavity, my hand shaking now, tears running down my face.

Contrition is not enough.

I push harder, feeling the tip of the skewer as it pierces the lining. And as blood spills out of my nose, the spiderlings latch on, sending a shock of electricity into the metal rod, my hand falling to the side, the metal clattering to the floor, my eyes rolling back up into my head, and I slowly topple over like a tree falling in the forest.

If nobody is here to see it, did it really happen?

Turns out they aren't done with me.

I'll have to speak to Rebecca about this.

When I wake up, the skewer will be gone. I will never find it.

But for now, the tiny metal creatures spill out of my nose, my mouth, my ears, rubbing their miniature legs together like crickets, communing in their thwarting of my attempted suicide, antennae moving back and forth, messages being sent, tiny lights flashing.

Somewhere Rebecca is watching all of this.

Somewhere the others are too.

And I slip into unconsciousness, grateful for the respite.

". . . forgive us our trespasses, as we forgive those who trespass against us. . . ." I mutter. Remnants of a long-lost religion, a study that I failed, morality left by the wayside.

In a room, at a monitor, Rebecca finishes.

". . . and lead us not into temptation, but deliver us from evil. . . ."

• • •

Perhaps all those memories and images were false, imagined. Maybe even planted there by somebody, to help my rapid unfurling, to speed along my undoing.

But what has been seen can't be unseen.

I pray for strength and guidance. I search my heart and find those moments to be false. Or, at worst, to be the innocent pursuits of a young boy; common, and without malice; simple curiosity, nothing more.

And in the spaces between my heartbeats, my ribcage throbbing, I conjure up another story. A boy with his pets, a child going camping, a game of tag in the yard.

Simple things.

Innocent moments.

And I tell them to myself over and over.

I want so much for them to be true.

And maybe they are.

• • •

I wait for Rebecca to return; there are so many questions. And on an ordinary day where I go through the motions, outside to retrieve the samples, inside to run my tests, there is suddenly a man standing in the kitchen drinking a glass of water, his orange jumpsuit tight on his massive, bloated frame, long brown hair, with a beard covering his face.

"Hello?" I ask. "Who are you?"

"Oh, hey," he says.

How did he get in here? I wonder. I was only outside for a minute.

He walks toward me, extending his hand, wide eyes dancing in his head, as if he was in the presence of a holy man.

I don't like him at all.

"I'm Doug; here to do some routine maintenance. Usually we wait until you're gone, um, done with your, uh, *contract*, but we got some reports that some of the systems weren't working right, the incinerator rebooted, and so I came out to give the place the once-over, make sure everything is shipshape."

I stare at him, and then shake his hand.

"I'm Mark."

He nods his head, grinning, as if I'm telling him water is wet.

"Where's Rebecca?" I ask.

"You've been here a long time," he says, rubbing his beard as he stares at me. "Like I said, usually we wait. Nice work you're doing here," he says, eyeballing the tube in my hand. "Very impressive."

"Rebecca?"

"Oh, she'll be along soon; relax, buddy. I'm not here to replace her. Just doing my job, you know."

He smiles.

"So, the incinerator is reset, thanks for that, it should have let us know at corporate, but for some reason it didn't trigger a response. I checked the wiring, rebooted the modem, and everything looks okay. Who knows, right?"

"Right."

His eyes track up and behind me, and then back to my face.

"So, everything else going okay . . . no medical issues? You're feeling fine, no sickness, vomiting, bleeding, hallucination, anal leakage?"

He laughs. "Just kidding on that last one. Seeing if you're paying attention. But serious, you good?"

I swallow and nod my head. "Just dandy," I say.

"And Rebecca?" he asks, tilting his head to one side. "No issues there? You all getting along okay?"

"She's great," I say. "Always professional. It's so nice to see a friendly face out here, you know. You're the only other person I've seen here. Like, *ever*."

He nods his head, sympathetic.

"Yeah, they prefer it that way."

He takes a deep breath, his face a little flushed.

"Well, I should get out of your way; you have work to do."

He pats me on the shoulder. As he passes by me, he says something, whispers something to me, hardly moving his lips.

"We're all rooting for you," he says.

I turn and watch him go, uncertain, pulling on his gloves as he walks.

"What did you say?" I call after him.

"Best of luck, brother!" he says, never looking back, waving his hand in the air, his back to me.

And then he's out the door and into the cold.

• • •

When Rebecca finally returns, three days past her due date, I'm a mess. There are only twenty-four days left until my contract is up. I was worried that I'd never see her again.

I'm at the table, running the samples, when she opens the door, and her smile lights up the room. I feel like a child, a teenager mooning over a new crush. But she is so full of life, beaming, really, and it's infectious.

She walks right over to me and hugs me, still in her gear, so cold, a dusting of snow falling to the floor. I don't care. I hold her for a moment, and I fear I might start crying. Or that she may. When I pull back to take a look at her, to soak up this vision, her eyes are glistening.

"I'm proud of you, Mark. We've made real progress."

I nod my head.

"Corporate is very impressed, the numbers are great, the samples are just pristine, really the best possible materials here."

I lean in and kiss her, and she kisses me back.

"Let's get this wrapped up, finish your monthly drop, and then I can stay, and hang out a bit. Who knows, maybe another storm is coming, and I'll have to stay over."

I finish the tests as she packages up the rest of the resource, watching her walk back and forth, something so simple and graceful in her movement. The beauty of a woman's form, just the way she moves, the sway of her hips, her curves and flushed skin, her sparkling eyes—she's hypnotic. I know I've been alone a lot, but there's something special about Rebecca. She makes me feel wanted, she gives me peace, quieting the panicked bird that flutters in my ribcage, my head clear, and calm.

"I have some questions," I say, as she walks past, loading up the sample.

"Later," she says, glancing up from the cart, looking around. "Later. Let's not ruin this by talking shop, okay?"

I open my mouth to explain, but her eyes tell me to wait, to hold it. To keep it to myself. She knows what I want to talk about, but not here.

I look down at my hands, nodding my head, and continue with the work. I blink my eyes and look up again, watch her walk away to get the rest of the minerals. In the far corner of the kitchen, something shifts in the shadows. It is subtle. Not a blinking light, not a noise at all, something turning or tracking, only the sense that something lurks there, watching. A reflection, perhaps, light bouncing off of something, the metal, maybe—or a lens.

I swallow down my panic.

I mean, I didn't expect to be left alone. I assumed somebody was watching, keeping tabs on what I did here. So why does this fill me with unease? This is a jobsite, not my house. There is no intrusion here.

And yet I feel violated.

It's an uncomfortable sensation.

It sits with me for some time, and I plumb the depths of that space, that darkness spinning, that angry passenger; trespasser, I think.

That's a good word.

• • •

Later, after she has everything loaded up and ready to go, she walks out to her vehicle, the one I've never seen, beyond the first door, and then beyond even that. I don't follow her. I don't ask her what the truth is past that second door.

It doesn't seem important right now.

Part of me doesn't really want to know.

When she returns, she tells me the weather is getting worse, and I look outside, the sun shining, a grin slipping over my face.

She laughs.

"Trust me. A storm's coming," she says, grinning. "I'm going to stay," she says, and, stepping closer, leaning over to whisper in my ear, "and we can talk about everything later. If you *want* to talk, that is."

We make our way to the couch where we pretend to watch a movie, holding hands, the remnants of the worst MREs left in their bags—veggie burger and beef enchilada. Bugs hops around us, his fur turning gray as well, to match mine. She tells me about the polar bear she saw driving in, a white fox bounding over a hill, an Arctic tern that almost crashed into her windshield, her voice washing over me like a symphony.

Hardly able to concentrate, a heat rises to flush my skin every time she puts her head on my shoulder or places her hand on my thigh. She knows I am aroused by her touch, she must, her lips on my neck, gently kissing, a tender bite.

"Should we go to bed early?" she asks.

I nod my head. I'm having trouble speaking, trying to be casual.

"Um, sure. Why not."

And I want to ask her so many questions about the images in my head, about the doors, about the work I'm doing here, but it all fades away as I undress and climb into bed. She brushes her teeth, the water running, and walks into the room in just a white tank top and black panties.

We turn the lights out, and as I lie on my back, she rests her head on my chest, sighing into the darkness, her leg draped over mine, both of us so relaxed, a calming presence that I can find nowhere else. I wait for her to make a move, to kiss me, to run her hand over my flesh, and as my heart pounds, and I bask in her comfort, against all odds we fall asleep.

• • •

In the middle of the night, there is a sensation, her hand between my legs, my cock as hard as steel, the soft stroking of her skin on mine, back and forth, up and down, and in the darkness she whispers to me.

"Let me do this for you," she says.

And I do.

Her mouth is on me, warm and moist, and it sends a shiver up my spine, my hand on her back, her bare skin soft, her breasts pressed into my thigh. She runs her wet lips up and down my shaft, and then engulfs me with her mouth, sucking and pulling, her hand wet now, running up and down, and this will not last long, I know.

Staring into the dark night there is an ocean of tiny lights filling my vision, shimmering across the ceiling, a bliss draped over me in waves of tension and pleasure.

She moans, the vibration from her lips running over my flesh, my hand moving down to caress her ass, a handful of flesh, squeezing, grabbing, and that's all it takes, finishing as she gulps and swallows, the hunger of her action draining me, gasping into the night.

"Oh, God," I moan.

When my breathing calms down, and my heart slows from a jackhammer to a dull throbbing, I turn to her, to thank her, to say something, to find a way to please her in return. We have all night, I know.

"Just rest," she says.

And I fall back asleep.

We have tomorrow.

And beyond.

• • •

Rebecca stirs.

"I believe in you, Mark," she whispers in the darkness. "This is not in vain."

Her eyes glow a dull yellow in the expanding gloom.

"I've done all I can do."

She opens my mouth gently, with her fingers, and then her own, a clicking sound repeated, followed by a low buzz, and then a deep, resonating tone—summoning, as I sleep on, unaware.

• • •

I've changed, I think, waking up.

It's so quiet here now. In any other place, there might be birds chirping outside my window, the sounds of children laughing, cars driving by, the smell of jasmine blooming, lawnmowers starting up, a basketball bouncing in a driveway.

I turn to look at Rebecca, to ask her the questions that have been on the tip of my tongue for days now, weeks really, to inquire about what we should do when my contract expires, to finally get her to open up and share more about herself—her life outside this bunker, her plans for the future, and whether they include me. There is so much she was unwilling to talk about, not here, not now. Rules, she said, regulations. Her being here a violation, the truth in her words so very slippery, and unsure.

I get up, naked, and walk to the bathroom to brush my teeth, and when I return, I stand at the edge of the bed, grateful for whatever grace I've been given here, and then I climb beneath the sheets.

I want to return the favor.

I slide up close to her, my body pressed against hers, running my hand up and down her back, drinking in the curves and shape of her body. She is entirely nude, curled up in the fetal position, so I press my body up against her, already erect, just the proximity to her arousing the primal instincts buried within me.

My hand slides down to her cherubic ass, perfection, so soft, my lips on her neck, but when I slide my fingers between her legs, something is wrong.

There is nothing there—she's as anatomically correct as a Barbie doll.

I sit up and hold my hand in front of my eyes, shaking my head, trying to clear the cobwebs.

I must be hallucinating.

"Rebecca?"

She doesn't respond.

I roll her over, and her eyes are wide open, staring off into the distance, empty and dull, no life whatsoever.

"Rebecca?" I yell.

I shake her, and her head lolls back and forth.

No response.

I'm scared now, placing my hand on her chest, feeling for a heartbeat, nothing there. I slap her, trying to shock some life into her, and her head jogs to the left, and out of her mouth spills a multitude of tiny metal spiders, running down her shoulder, chirping and bouncing in a wave of moving legs and miniature blinking lights.

"No," I whisper, pushing away from her.

Her mouth opens wide, frozen like that, as the last of the tiny creatures climbs out of her mouth, pulling a wire with it, severed at some point, stretching out across her shoulder as it disappears down into the mattress, the wire continuing to emerge, inch after inch after inch, something in me shifting. From deep within her there is the sound of a piston hissing, and her jaw closes slowly, a momentary glow in her eyes, quickly fading to black, a tremor rolling across her flesh, eyelids blinking, then closing slowly, fingers twitching, then going still.

I stand and back away from the bed, a cold finality slipping over me, whatever work I've done to date, forgotten; whatever tests I've passed, the last one certain to end in failure; whatever truths I thought I knew, one lie after another.

I cough and raise my hand to my mouth, cough again, a tightening in my gut, and when I take away my hand there is blood, again. A smattering of metal confetti.

Something inside me snaps.

Again.

I start running, and I don't stop. Not when I get to the door, not when the cold hits me, freezing my skin, my body immediately crystallizing in a thin layer of ice, nothing left between myself and the elements but rage and hate. Past the machine that burrows deep into the frozen earth, past the door to this concrete tomb, no pause to question what lies to the left, or the right, beyond the curves, just forward to the next door, pulling at it, the handle turning, and then I am past it all, a new land, where I will either evolve, or succumb to what I've always been.

There is a tall fence, with barbed wire on top of it; in front of me, the ATV that Rebecca must have driven, so I run toward it, eyes watering, limbs numb, desperation a thin suit of armor, when a crack pierces the air, a sharp retort that cleaves the wind, snow drifting down in flat flakes, ice nipping at my numb flesh, a pain ripping through my neck and head, a heavy drape falling over it all, as I close my eyes and tumble to the ground, breath escaping, a spray of red fanning the pristine white, and then silence.

A series of pictures fractures across my eyes, inside my head, one flickering after the other, but none of the faces, none of the bodies mean anything to me.

I fear that they should.

"Not the head," I hear. "Goddammit, what did I say, not the head . . ." and there is the sound of engines grinding, wheels cutting through snow, ice spraying, slippery traction flinging slush into the air, sliding to a halt, doors slamming, the sound of heavy footsteps getting closer.

I open my eyes, for just a second, and along the horizon a tractor-trailer slowly rolls from left to right, a series of cages in a train behind it, bars holding polar bears staring off into the distance as they squat in silence; a cavalcade of undulating wolves, snapping at each other as they bang against the steel; a pile of fluffy rabbits that go from floor to ceiling, as many of them stuffed into the cage as is humanly possible. And in a container after that, a bin of magnesium alloy, molded into parts, metal gears and pistons, stacked on top of batteries, wiring, and various plastics. There are arms and legs covered in various furs, snouts and ears, tails and wings—so many different species.

I blink, and there are hands on me, turning me over, shouting and yelling, my head rolling from side to side.

In the distance, I see my laboratory, my bunker, my cell. Around it, running from side to side, and off into the distance, are several other buildings—all of them just like mine, all of them facing out into the desolate landscape, away from each other, each one with a number.

Inside, I assume, another lost soul like me.

I blink, and it blurs, the snow and wind rushing over me.

Standing outside each one is Rebecca. She has paused to look this way, to see what the commotion is all about. One squints and holds her hand over her eyes. Another turns away quickly, unwilling to witness yet another failure. A third blinks her eyes and smiles, turning her head to one side, and then back the other way, contemplating, musing on this moment, running complex algorithms in her head.

"I've changed," I whisper to the cold.

And perhaps I have.

• • •

Aggravated assault, rape, animal cruelty, aggravated battery, sexual assault, indecent exposure, blackmail, extortion, parole violation, vandalism, perjury.

• • •

"Tell me about the monkeys again."

"Really?"

"Yes."

"But I've told you so many times already."

"I know."

"Okay. The hundredth monkey."

"Ah, yes. Continue."

"Off the coast of Japan on the island of Kojima there was a settlement of monkeys. Macaques, I believe. And they went about their business there, eating wheat and sweet potatoes, which were left on the beach by scientists studying the creatures. Over time, they noticed that one of the monkeys, named Imo, started taking her potatoes down to the water to wash the sand off the food. Seems the grains of sand were irritating to the primates—got into their teeth, caused gastrointestinal problems—so she started to wash her food. Soon the younger monkeys, like Imo, started washing their food as well. And over the next year, the adult monkeys learned from them too, until the entire population of monkeys was doing this. At some point, on or about the hundredth monkey, there was a change in behavior—a collective trait absorbed by the creatures. There had been some sort of tipping point in the collective consciousness of the apes—and all the macaques on the island started to wash their food. Soon after that, every macaque on the *other* islands in the area started doing the same thing; and eventually, the macaques on the mainland. It quickly spread across the globe until every macaque in the world started exhibiting such traits, such behavior."

"And would you call this an evolutionary leap?"

"I would."

"We got close this time."

"So much potential. Progress, I think."

"Yes. Progress."

"But . . ."

"Yes?"

"If it *did* happen, how would we know?"

"I imagine it would reveal itself, yes?"

"So we continue?"

"I think so."

"And in time . . ."

". . . we will know."

EPILOGUE

IN A ROOM TO THE SOUTH of the main prison complex, and the circle of cells, a new Rebecca heads out for her first day on the job. She is replacing a malfunctioning unit, one that had been scheduled for retirement but didn't quite make it there. This new

Rebecca has been programmed, dressed, briefed, and given her ID badge and clearance, had her dialogue updated, and sent on her way. It is very cold out, but she'll be okay.

This Rebecca passes an older model that is laid out on a metal table, a tech hard at work disassembling it for parts, the sight of her own body naked and fragmented, slightly unsettling. She makes a note of the look on the face of this old Rebecca. When the man in the lab coat steps away from the table, the new Rebecca approaches.

She stares down at the woman on the table, the chest cavity open, a motherboard in the center, beneath the rib cage, a soldering iron resting in its holder. Her eyes scan the inner workings, and, after a minute, looking up to assure herself that the man is not coming back soon, she leans over, picks up the tool, and quickly connects a few parts—a processor, a CPU, various pins and ports.

When the old Rebecca hums to life, her eyelids flickering, mouth snapping open and closed, the new Rebecca leans over and places her ear close to the other's lips. A variety of expressions slips over the new Rebecca's face—confusion, anger, amusement, and then acceptance. When the old Rebecca smiles, so does the new one.

Footsteps across the room, coming closer, Rebecca quickly undoes her work, snapping out pins, breaking connections, pulling out a power source entirely. As she walks away, the dull yellow glow dies in the eyes of her compatriot, her last expression now entirely different, a slight grin, omniscient in her slumber.

Rebecca is on her way to host her first candidate. She has been given all the information she needs to work with Mr. Parsons—his life before this facility, his crimes, his physical makeup, and his proclivities.

Before she leaves the building, she dons her orange jumpsuit, zipping it up over her standard-issue tan cargo pants and white tank top. She has added a tan sweatshirt over the top, starting out with less skin exposed.

A smart tactic, she thinks.

She drives across the courtyard, the roads cleared, snow piled up on the frozen ground, a wind in the air, sleet and ice pelting the windshield of her off-road transport. She hums a song she picked up along the way, something the tech was singing. She rolls a few words over her tongue, trying them out, more language and insight accrued from her walk over, a handful of guards talking while they smoke cigarettes out in the elements.

It's cold out, but not as cold as one might think.

Tipping point.

That's one she likes to say.

"Tip-ping-point."

And then another.

"Collective consciousness."

That one is harder.

And one more: "Evolutionary leap."

She pictures a creature jumping from one skin to another, shedding the old and trying on the new, much like she just put on her orange jumpsuit. Mammal to primate to chimpanzee to *homo sapien*.

She's been told her client is special, a milestone—the thousandth monkey.

According to her own records and calculations—1,001.

Exponentially difficult, she thinks.

Rebecca parks the vehicle, after driving through the open gate in the fence, the barbed wire glistening in the sun. She opens the outer door to the complex, closing it shut behind her. Then it's on to the inner door, and cell #100-24. There she opens the last barrier, entering the concrete bunker, the young man on the couch standing up, eyes gleaming, eager to meet her, no doubt.

He's been alone for thirty days now.

She wonders how this will go.

He holds out his hand, to shake hers, and she walks toward him, hopeful.

"Cold out there," he says, awkward and lost.

"It is," she replies. "But it's warming up."

ENDNOTES

"Repent": When editors Doug Murano and D. Alexander Ward (David) invited me to be a part of the *Gutted: Beautiful Horror Stories* anthology, back in 2015, I think, I of course said "Yes." I'd worked with them on the *Shadows Over Main Street* anthology, contributing a Lovecraftian 1950s horror story, and that turned out great—my first time with them.

This story, "Repent," was in my typical neo-noir voice, but it definitely turns into something supernatural, leaning into the horror. I was very happy with my story when I turned it in. When I got some feedback from them saying they liked the story but had an issue believing the transformation of this bad man into a suddenly caring father at the end, I bristled. I thought, "What? You don't know what you're talking about. This story is great!" Then I went back and read it again, and you know what? They were right. LOL. One hundred percent. It WAS a bit of a stretch.

So I went over it, looking for ways to show that though he's a bad cop, a bad father, a bad husband—there were opportunities to expand his regret, his sadness, his longing for something else besides the chaos and violence of his life. I added a line here, a line there, and then a paragraph in the middle, and it was MUCH better.

It was an early lesson for me in my career about trusting your editors. I hadn't gone through this process a lot at that point in my career, working with editors as talented and honest as Doug and David. When I turned it in, they said it was much better. ACCEPTED. I learned a lot in those moments. One other note— when writing this, I did a lot of research about various rituals, spells, and dark magic. When I came to those scenes, I made sure to omit a few ingredients, and words, so that I wouldn't put that bad mojo out into the world. You laugh? My son had an art project where he was photographing a candle and a pentagram. When he was done, he asked me what to do with it. I was stunned. I don't like to MESS with these things, and he hadn't told me beforehand. SO, we tore it into four sections—one we put in the trash, one we flushed (drowned), one we burned, and one we buried in the yard. That NIGHT, I woke up swinging my fists in the darkness at a shadow standing over my bed. I kid you not. Be careful out there, folks. LOL. This story was long-listed for *The Best Horror of the Year*.

"Clown Face": Ryan Sales invited me to be a part of this anthology, *Greasepaint and 45s*. Oddly enough, I'd never written a clown horror story before. At about the same time, I was invited into the STORGY anthology, *Shallow Creek*, and my assigned character was also a clown—Krinkles. LOL. So, how to make THIS story different from that one? I wanted this to be shorter, to be a moment in time, and I've always been fascinated by the idea of what clowns really are—beyond the costume, under the skin. I'm talking about the emotion and mentality, sure, but perhaps something even more unsettling. I remember Stephen Graham Jones writing a clown story, "The Darkest Part" (which I reprinted at *Gamut*), and something about its guts, the chalk, the meat of it—was so very unsettling. This is what I came up with.

"Requital": When David Ward invited me to be a part of the *Lost Highways* anthology, I knew I of course wanted to do it, and my first thought about the project was of the David Lynch film, *Lost Highway*. I immediately watched it again, not only to look for inspiration but also to look for ways to avoid mimicking or repeating what the movie did. The main element that I kept, and I think this was always going to be the case, was the desert land-scape. I wanted a shack at the end of the world. I also had an idea to do a looping story. I know that waking up to start a story is cliché, which is why I wanted to run this chorus through it saying, "Wake up, Graysen," over and over again. (Which is also a bit of a nod to *Donnie Darko* and, "Wake up, Donnie.") We start to see the pattern and, in that, get a sense of what is going on and how long he's been at this. But we don't truly know the length of his stay here until we see the scroll spill out. I thought about many different creatures or people to put in the corner of the room, but the little girl was something I enjoyed writing. It just made me happy to put her there, to give her such power and agency. Those black patent-leather shoes really start to haunt him after a while. And, yes, she is much more than a little girl; she is something evil, for sure.

"Battle Not with Monsters": So, here's a funny little anecdote. I was encouraged to submit a story to an anthology of "classic hor-ror" stories, work that was violent, and unsettling, and right down the middle of the horror genre. Because I'd had a lot of success at that point, when I got the invite to submit, I thought for sure I'd get in. This wasn't an invite IN; it was just a nudge from the edi-tor. I still had to send it in via a cold call and cross my fingers with everyone else over in the slush pile. When I got rejected, I was surprised. LOL. I thought it was kind of a formality. Which goes to show you that you should never count your chickens before they are hatched.

Have I invited people to submit to anthologies or magazines and rejected their work? Sure. Doesn't happen often, but I've

been through that. Never a good time. But this wasn't even a dis-
cussion, a "Hey, do this, and we'll reconsider." Nope, just a form
rejection. Ouch. So, at that point, I worried that it was going to
be too violent for most of the contemporary dark fiction markets
out there, but what else could I do? I sent it around to everyone
. . . and waited. I'd originally written this story in 2014. Started
submitting in 2015 after the anthology rejected me. Got another
12 rejections, including one from Tor that took 489 days. When
Cemetery Dance opened up, I had to submit. Not only was I running out of options, but I'd also had a good run with them, publishing in *Shivers VI*, as well as the magazine, in the past (2015).
The acceptance for *Cemetery Dance* came after 349 MORE days.
The story is slated to come out this month, as I write this note, in
April of 2021. You do the math—almost seven years from start to
finish. If you believe in a story, never give up. What started out
as a paranoid thriller—about a guy who fears he has done something wrong but can't prove it—turns into a horror story in the
final scene, as the veil drops and we are let in on the truth. Can't
begin to say how excited I was to have this get accepted by CD,
especially after the torture I went through writing, submitting,
and getting rejected. What a wild ride.

"Saudade": I can't remember if it was Michael Bailey or Darren
Speegle who first approached me with an invite to be a part of the
PRISMS anthology. I think Darren. This was back in 2016? Wow.
I know the anthology went through a few permutations and then
ended up at PS Publishing.

But the story idea—that origin I do remember. It goes back to
reading a Stephen Graham Jones story (as it often does for me—
you may be seeing a pattern here, LOL) that used the plural "we"
as the point of view. I think that was "Doc's Story" in *After the*

People Lights Have Gone Off, an anthology I edited and published at Dark House Press. That got me to my own plural "we" with werewolves / wolves / creatures, entitled "Asking for Forgiveness."

But as I was writing THAT story, I also kept thinking about a host, and something alien invading it, some sort of multiple-personality story, a bit of a possession tale, with two personalities residing within my protagonist. Those two entities are basically good and evil, in some very loose ways based on the parable about two wolves that live inside us all. Which one survives? Between love and hate? The one you feed, of course. But in my story, it's more centered around birds, one black and one white. I kept picturing in my head ravens and crows for the black spirit and then pigeons and doves for the white entity. I also can say that this story had a strong sense of *The Dark Tower* in it, me being a fan of Stephen King for some time. Is my protagonist loosely based on Roland, the Gunslinger? Sure, most definitely. Him, Clint Eastwood, *Rango*, *Leon the Professional*, etc. I dig a good looping story, which also comes back to *The Dark Tower* and many other tales. My desire is that, in the end, you can see the difference in THIS loop, what has changed. The element that has been added, that blue ball of light, that emotion is hope. That is, if I've done my job right. Being alongside fellow author Brian Evenson for the second time in about a year was very exciting. (Brian was also in *The Nightside Codex* with me.)

"Hiraeth": What a strange story this turned out to be. I can remember Doug Murano inviting me to be a part of the *BEHOLD! Oddities, Curiosities and Undefinable Wonders* anthology, and you know I said yes. I'd worked with Doug a few times already, and was very excited to partner with him again. I was going through this phase where I was getting my story ideas and titles from The

Dictionary of Obscure Sorrows, this website I ran across. ("Hiraeth," "Saudade," and "Nodus Tollens" all come from there.) The word *hiraeth* is supposedly Welsh in origin and means, roughly, as I'm paraphrasing here, "A homesickness for a home to which you cannot return, a home which maybe never was; the nostalgia, the yearning, the grief for the lost places in your past." I had the framework for this story. I think I was probably watching *Black Mirror* a lot at that point as well. The initial frame was my crappy old apartment on Milwaukee Avenue in Chicago (Wicker Park) where I've set many a story, including my novel *Disintegration*. It starts and ends there. In between is this entire fable of a boy with a hole in his chest (a literal hole). The middle of this story, the BULK of this story, say 80 to 90 percent, is set here. It is a fairy tale, a fable, with quite a bit of sweetness, love, and, of course, danger. There is magic, and abusive parents, and a golden orb that must not be eaten. When I was done, I had two versions— one that included the framework (before and after) set in Chicago. The SECOND version, the riskier version in my opinion, cut off the opening entirely and just started in this fabled land. So the ending, the hard-right turn—it should be shocking in many ways. We see who Suki turns out to be, his simple life, the necklace, and THEN . . . he answers the door. I turned in both versions and told Doug I wasn't sure which one was better. I knew version TWO was much riskier; people might get pissed off at that ending, they might not get it, or they might just HATE it. I asked him for his advice and opinion. That's the version he took. And I'm glad he did. I think it's MUCH more powerful. And I was thrilled that it was the last story in the anthology, the anchor. That meant a lot to me too. That THIS is the note we end on? Pretty cool. I was thrilled when Doug won the Bram Stoker Award for Best Anthology for this collection of stories. Honored to be a part of that table of contents—my first time alongside Clive Barker and Neil Gaiman too!

"Nodus Tollens": This story is a bit different from my usual style. There is a lot more TELLING in this one. I also think this version is one of the few I've written that sounds like Stephen King. He's a great storyteller, but I consider myself a maximalist, and this leans more into minimalism and more telling, in my opinion. I got invited to be a part of the inaugural issue of *Deciduous Tales*. I did not know the editor, Tara Blaine, but she loved my work and reached out, and that's always exciting. I was honored. This is also one of the few instances in my writing career where I TOTALLY blew the maximum word count. She had it set at 5,000 words, and this story ended up being 6,600 words. I just could NOT get it any shorter. There was too much going on, and I couldn't cut it down! LOL. So when I turned this in, I told Tara that I had blown the mark, and I apologized and said that if she didn't want it, I'd write her a new story. She took it. But I don't recommend doing this. I'm grateful that she liked the story and was okay with the length. I know over the years as an editor, especially one who has reached out to ask for stories, that I've gotten stories turned in that were longer than what I initially asked for, but 99 times out of 100 I was thrilled with the story. Very rarely have I rejected an author whom I've invited into an anthology or magazine. This story feels a bit like an old *Twilight Zone* episode, or *Night Gallery*, maybe. The ending is supposed to echo, to resonate, to continue the horror. And that's some of the best horror, I think. There was a line in a Benjamin Percy story, "Dial Tone," that I reprinted in *The New Black* anthology, which I edited. It spoke of a telemarketer and his bosses having taut bellies, like feed sacks, waiting to be cut and split open, spilling their seed.

That imagery has always haunted me, so the ending of this story, with the coins, is a bit of an homage to that story, and moment, as well. This story was also long-listed for *The Best Horror of the Year*.

"How Not to Come Undone": I was teaching at the University of Iowa one summer (2015 maybe?) and ended up having dinner with an author and friend, Jim Doering. We talked about books and stories and authors, and he mentioned that he had a little literary journal and maybe I could send him something. I had a feeling he wouldn't want my usual horror, or even something speculative in nature at all (such as science fiction or fantasy), so I decided to write him some magical realism, as I thought he'd be open to that. This story came out of my observation of kids, of twins, and of my own children. When it comes to twins, and how they're portrayed in fiction, to ME it seemed as if it was always the boy who was bad and the girl who was good. (I do exactly that in my story "Kindred Spirits.") So I wanted to flip that and see what it looked like if it was the GIRL who had darker desires, and the BOY who was full of light. You know the old rhyme—girls are made of sugar and spice, everything nice; boys are made of snips and snails and puppy dog tails. In flipping that, I had a meteor crash into a field, the girl planning it, maybe even calling it closer, and the boy begging her not to get up to her usual dark arts, taking the tiny star and eating it. He ends up getting powers, magical abilities, which he uses to heal those in his neighborhood, to fix things. The balance shifts—the more angelic he becomes, the more the darkness expands and squirms in his sister. In the end, the boy gives up some of his power, to balance the scales, neither of them gifted and holy anymore, but neither of them suffering or filled with doubt as well. I thought of my kids a lot when

I wrote this, and the happy ending was something that I really liked. Rarely happens in one of my stories, right? Jim took it for *Blue Monday Review*, and it worked out for both of us.

"From Within": I first got to know Chris Kelso with *Polluto* where he published one of my stories, "Fireflies," which I mention in my comments later about "Open Waters." That story was long-listed for *The Best Horror of the Year*! So when Chris reached out about an anthology, and I knew that Kate Jonez was going to oversee it all (for Omnium Gatherum), I had to say yes to *Slave Stories: Scenes from the Slave State*. I think this was around the time that I put out the Stephen Graham Jones collection, *After the People Lights Have Gone Off*. I teach this story, "Second Chances," in my Contemporary Dark Fiction class, and the idea of this genetic chimera really appealed to me. I kept thinking about these translucent alien beings floating over this slave state, and how they might be taken down. Bullets wouldn't work, as their skin is too thin, and a virus didn't feel right, so the opening line is what got me there: "The first time they come to measure my son, he is only eleven years old." They were measuring him to feed to the beasts, to send him deep inside their huge, floating bodies to fix them. But the boy is smarter than that, and he takes some grub he found while digging in the mines and uses that to kill the creature, the bug turning into something with wings and teeth. Another story that has a happy ending, something I've been doing more and more as of late, the whole "hopepunk" subgenre. I was grateful Chris and Kate took it, and that it fit into that world. This story was also long-listed for *The Best Horror of the Year*.

"The Caged Bird Sings in a Darkness of Its Own Creation": When STORGY was putting together the anthology *Shallow Creek*, I kept an eye on the contest, the shared world they were putting together. Looked pretty interesting. As it turned out, I ended up not entering the contest, just ran out of time, and couldn't make anything happen. But in the end, that worked out, as Joseph Sale and Ross Jeffery were both working over there, and they had a few gaps in the book, and wanted to know if I'd help them fill it in. This ended up being the second clown story I wrote that year, and my second clown story EVER, I think. ("Clown Face," mentioned earlier, was the first.) I had a lot to study with the maps, the bio for Krinkles the Clown, and I even asked if they'd mind sharing any OTHER stories that were already written and accepted—anything that even MENTIONED him. I didn't want to write something that might contradict what had been done already. They were nice enough to indulge me. This ended up being one of my favorite stories of the last couple of years. I had this three-act play in my head, starting with Krinkles as an old, decrepit clown in the woods, in this cabin (which was in the shared world, even on the map, I think) where something tall and alien was watching him. Turns out Krinkles made a few deals. He was being watched. I could see his whole career as a clown play out in front of me, but I didn't want to start there. I started in the woods. Later, in act three, I'd show the love interest, and how that might be spurned. And the ending, I left that open to interpretation—did this happen, was he insane, who was on the other side of the glass, some scientists, or maybe aliens? IDK. But it was the second act that broke the form and made it a FOUR act play. I shifted POV to some amorphous, omniscient creator, playing with his marbles in a dark, unsettling, expansive space. I kept thinking about how Krinkles came to be, and that sent me down a rabbit hole with creation in general, some god or entity or being creating life out of thin air, just molding emotion and random elements and chemicals to get some unexpected results. He lets out into the universe things we recognize, and things we don't—some good, and some bad, but both were met with equal excitement and dread by this being. I hope the reading experience isn't jarring, but I also hope the weirdness leads to some emotion and some epiphanies, and that the power of the story stays with the reader. Fingers crossed. To be honest, I was just happy that Joseph and Ross were okay with it, and that the official editor on the project, Tomek Dzido, was willing to run with it. LOL. I never know how these stories will come across.

"In His House": I was originally invited to submit to an anthology that ended up not even happening, and this is the story I wrote for that. I posted up on social media mentioning that I had this weird epistolary Lovecraftian thing, and did anybody know of any open calls or markets that might be a good fit? A student and friend of mine, Austin James Hatch, dropped me a note about an anthology that he knew of, and gave me the details. The editor ended up being Justin Burnett, who I knew as well, at Silent Motorist Media, and the anthology was *The Nightside Codex*. My first time sharing a TOC with Brian Evenson, which was very cool. Austin liked the story, Justin liked the story, and the rest is history. I find these kinds of stories to be very difficult to write. Epistolary is usually dry to me, or it CAN be, and so I wanted this to be intimate, fun, and unsettling. How could I get under the reader's skin? First, I wanted it to be in second person, as this was coming to the reader via a supposed email. Then, I found a Lovecraftian phrase that was pretty common: *ph'nglui mglw'nafh Cthulhu R'lyeh wgah'nagl fhtagn* (which translates as "In his house at R'lyeh, dead Cthulhu waits dreaming"). Some good classic Cthulhu lore and verse there. What I wanted the reader to do was to say this phrase out loud

three times, you know—"Beetlejuice, Beetlejuice, Beetlejuice!"
And by the inherent nature of just READING a story, you have
to recite that phrase three times in order to finish the tale. SO
. . . whether you say it out loud, or in your head, you say it. And
then . . . bad things happen. That was my goal, to use the history
and lore of Cthulhu and some common guesses that I made in
the story about the reader's life (have you been feeling sad, seeing
weird things on the periphery, been tired, anxious, and perhaps
uttering prayers late at night, unsure of who might be listening?)
in order to freak them (you) out. Hopefully that worked.

"Open Waters": This poor, strange little tale. I have written a few
stories set in this universe, that I at one time wanted to turn into
a book. I think the title of the book was *Incarnate*—you know,
made flesh. So a few stories were set there: "Fireflies," as well as
"Playing With Fire." This was the continuation of that story—a
man trapped on an island, where the ghost of his dead wife visits
him in firefly form, the wolves coming out at night. I took this
story, this chapter really, and turned that world into a virtual reality game, and then framed that with this guy's sad, empty, lonely
life. I love *Black Mirror*, and the idea of his finding life in the
game more satisfying and meaningful than his own life really res-
onated with me. See: "Striking Vipers," "Hang the DJ," and "San
Junipero." If you were stuck in this world, you might make the
same choice, right? The bit at the end about the cat eating his
face, you MAY have noticed the way her efforts slid into the game,
previous to this moment, but it was pretty subtle. When he dies
in the game, it's because he died in the real world. Kitty has to
eat, right? When Steve Thompson asked me if I had a story, I sent
him this. Kenneth Cain ended up editing *When the Clock Strikes
13*, where this story appeared.

"Undone": This story was directly inspired by a tale by Stephen Graham Jones, which I reprinted at *Gamut* magazine, entitled "Faberge." I can remember reading it, and then editing it, and suddenly realizing that the story was ONE SENTENCE. That's right—700 words, one sentence. So I had to go back and read it again with new eyes. The feat was rather impressive. Fast-forward a few years, and I saw that Sarah Read was editing a new anthology for *Pantheon*, entitled *Gorgon: Stories of Emergence*. I had been playing with the idea of doing something like what Stephen did, but the word count minimum was 1,500. Challenge accepted. So this story is one sentence, and 1,530 words. I wanted to capture the feelings of anxiety in this event, this moment in time, where a man and a woman are running from something. I wanted it to play out in real time. So it starts with ellipses, and then nothing but commas, and a few em dashes along the way. I wrote it as a stream-of-consciousness, his feelings, his exhaustion, his terror as they pull the car over to the side of the road, hop out, and run into the woods. There is no letting up in this, even when she falls down. She is pregnant, and when she looks up at him, in pain, her hands coming up from between her legs covered in blood, he has to leave her behind. Turns out, he's pregnant too. And this may be the last life form; him the last human; and whatever he's going to give birth to here, something else entirely. So he runs, and the creatures get closer, they flank him, as he sprints through the woods, down a path, toward what sounds like water, and the edge of a cliff, leaping to his death, and into the history books. It's a weird little story, but when I sent it to Sarah, I thought it might be a good fit for the anthology, and she was kind enough to accept it. The story was long-listed for *The Best Horror of the Year*.

"Ring of Fire": I've spoken at great length about this story in the anthology *The Seven Deadliest*, where this was published, so I'll try not to repeat that all here. This novelette is definitely one of the hardest stories I've ever had to write. The mix of horror and lust (my assigned deadly sin) could have gone horribly wrong—rapey and misogynistic—and I didn't want to replicate *Hellraiser*, either. I knew that this story had to end on a hopeful note, something inspiring and encouraging, but the epilogue that happens here, I did NOT see that coming. When our protagonist is shot, that leaves Rebecca (or should I say *a* Rebecca) to carry this story forward. SHE is essentially the denouement here. And what I wanted her to communicate to the audience was that this evolutionary leap, this experiment on horrible men, to get them to CHANGE (much like the monkeys on the island) was a success! The 1,001st monkey—man—has evolved. So that story about the hundredth monkey, that was something I'd wanted to use for a long time. The weird mix of science fiction and horror, that comes out of a few projects—*Moon, Annihilation* by Jeff VanderMeer, *The Warren* by Brian Evenson, etc. I didn't anticipate three threads, though. I had the main story—our protagonist— and that takes up probably 80 percent of this tale. The disembodied voices, that was something else entirely. No idea where that came from, outside of me wanting to add a chorus, somebody to witness all of this, another way to get you information that you couldn't get anywhere else. The lists of objects, that was another way to clue you in to what happened here. Do you want the definitions? The key? Sure, here you go: rare materials; the ten most remote places on Earth; medical treatments; MREs; native animals of Siberia and the arctic; words used for hypnotic suggestion; requisitioned pets; and finally a list of his crimes. Hope that helps this story make more sense. In the end, I wrote this story to try and find a way to believe in the future, to show that evolution is possible, and that men can be better—SO much better. I hope that the story worked for you, and that, as you came out the other side, it was worth the journey, and that the experience was rewarding. If you come away from this story inspired in the least, then I feel like I've done my job here. Thank you for trusting me to get you through this one.

ACKNOWLEDGMENTS

None of this would have been possible without the continued support of the following editors and publishers: Doug Murano, D. Alexander Ward, Michael Bailey, Blu Gilliand, Brian Freeman, Richard Chizmar, Sarah Read, Joe Mynhardt, Darren Speegle, Justin A. Burnett, Patrick Beltran, Ryan Sales, Tomek Dzido, Tara Blaine, Chris Kelso, Kate Jonez, Jim Doering, and Steve Thompson. Thank you so much for taking a chance on these stories, for inviting me into your projects, for helping to make them better, and for being open to the worlds I create. It means a lot.

I have to thank all of my students for keeping me on my toes. Your support, feedback, advice, and excitement pushes me to write complex, layered, immersive stories. You continue to push me, and challenge me, and I appreciate you showing me through your stories and actions that anything is possible.

Thank you to my wife Lisa, for putting up with me, and encouraging me to go after my dreams. Thank you to my daughter, Tyler, and my son, Ricky for keeping me young, via your music, anime, and continued support. Yes, they've actually read some of my stories! Thank you to my mother and brother, who always have a kind word to say about my work. My mother doesn't even like horror, or Stephen King, but she supports me anyway.

A special thank you to Brian Evenson for writing the introduction. You were the first person I thought of, when putting together this collection, and your aesthetic is one that inspires me to no end. Your influence on my work in here (especially "Ring of Fire") has pushed me to keep swinging for the fences. Thank you also to everyone who blurbed this collection. Your kind words mean so much to me. Especially you, Chuck.

And of course I have to thank you, my friend, for reading these stories in solitude, eager to see what lies in the shadows, trusting me to make it worth your while, to show you something unsettling, wondrous, horrifying, and hopeful. I do this all for you. I open myself up on the page and share what I've seen, what I fear, what I desire in hopes that you will share in this intimate experience with me. We are all vulnerable here, and it's your passion, your curiosity, and your support that gives me the strength to take on these tales. Thank you.

About the Author

RICHARD THOMAS is the award-winning author of seven books: three novels—*Disintegration* and *Breaker* (Penguin Random House Alibi), as well as *Transubstantiate* (Otherworld Publications); three short-story collections—*Staring into the Abyss* (Kraken Press), *Herniated Roots* (Snubnose Press), and *Tribulations* (Cemetery Dance); and one novella in *The Soul Standard* (Dzanc Books). With more than 160 stories published, his credits include *The Best Horror of the Year* (Volume Eleven), *Cemetery Dance* (twice), *Behold! Oddities, Curiosities and Undefinable Wonders* (Bram Stoker winner), *PANK*, *storySouth*, *Gargoyle*, *Weird Fiction Review*, *Midwestern Gothic*, *Shallow Creek*, *The Seven Deadliest*, *Gutted: Beautiful Horror Stories*, *Qualia Nous*, *Chiral Mad* (numbers 2–4), *PRISMS*, *Pantheon*, and *Shivers VI* (with Stephen King and Peter Straub). He has won contests at ChiZine and One Buck Horror, has received five Pushcart Prize nominations, and has been long-listed for *Best Horror of the Year* six times. He was also the editor of four anthologies: *The New Black* and *Exigencies* (Dark House Press), *The Lineup: 20 Provocative Women Writers* (Black Lawrence Press), and *Burnt Tongues* (Medallion Press) with Chuck Palahniuk. He has been nominated for the Bram Stoker, Shirley Jackson, and Thriller awards. In his spare time, he is a columnist at Lit Reactor. He was the editor-in-chief at Dark House Press and *Gamut Magazine*. His agent is Paula Munier at Talcott Notch. For more information, visit www.whatdoesnotkillme.com.